"Oh, Marsh—!"

He gathered her to him in a hard hug. "You *are* all right? He didn't hurt you—? If he did, I swear I'll—As it is, I'm not leaving here until he gets what he deserves!"

"Just take me home!" Vivi begged. "Marsh, please—don't cause a scene! He isn't worth it, and you—your ankle—"

For the first time, she realized he wasn't using his crutches. She drew back, staring up at his face, then down at his ankle.

"Marsh Henderson, you can walk perfectly well!" she accused, brown eyes stormy. "And you drove your own car down here—didn't you? How long have you been lying to me? Was it fun, making a fool out of me?"

Dear Reader,

The Promise Romance™ you are about to read is a special kind of romance written with you in mind. It combines the thrill of newfound romance and the inspiration of a shared faith. By combining the two, we offer you an alternative to promiscuity and superficial relationships. Now you can read a romantic novel—with the romance left intact.

Promise Romances™ will introduce you to exciting places and to men and women very much involved in today's fast-paced world, yet searching for romance and love with commitment—for the fulfillment of love's promise. You will enjoy sharing their experiences. Most of all you will be uplifted by a romance that involves much more than physical attraction.

Welcome to the world of Promise Romance™— a special kind of place with a special kind of love.

Etta Wilson

Etta Wilson, Editor

Bridge to Love

Fran Priddy

Promise Romances™

Thomas Nelson Publishers • Nashville • Camden • New York

Special thanks to the Covered Bridge Festival in Rockville, Parke County, Indiana, which I have loved for years, and to Charles Cole, who played his dulcimers and sang several of his songs so I could record them for mention in this story.

Published in Nashville, Tennessee, by Thomas Nelson, Inc. and distributed in Canada by Lawson Falle, Ltd., Cambridge, Ontario.

Unless otherwise noted, the Bible version used in this publication is The New English Bible, used by permission of the Delegates of the Oxford University Press and the Syndics of the Cambridge University Press, copyright 1961 and 1970.

Printed in the United States of America.

ISBN 0-8407-7371-4

To Helen Priddy
My mother and good friend

Chapter One

Vivi's eyes widened, then sparkled, at the sight in the driveway.

A scarlet Corvette Sting Ray was definitely incongruous outside Gran's big old white Victorian house.

She drew her own subcompact Ford Fiesta to a halt right behind it, thinking ruefully that the sole point of similarity was color. Both cars were bright red.

Vivi got out and stretched, the autumn breeze ruffling her short, curly dark hair before she reached to pull her possessions out. The slam of a screendoor made her turn with a smile of anticipation.

A small elderly woman beaming a welcome came hurrying down the steps to greet her. The resemblance between them was obvious despite the fifty-year age difference. Once Gran's silver hair had been dark as Vivi's, and it was still as curly, if not as recently styled. They had the same heart-shaped, vivid faces with large brown eyes. Gran's trim slacks and blue-plaid woven top and Vivi's jeans and scarlet T-shirt complemented the small, slim builds and quick, vital movements of the two delighted women.

"Granny!" she called. "I see you've got a new car!"

"Well, mercy, I've got to have some way to get to church Sundays, don't I?" Gran retorted. "The Buick was getting old and acting up!"

They hugged one another and laughed, enjoying the mental picture of Gran zipping around Rockville in a red sports car. That was even more incongruous than its presence outside her big old house—though Vivi wouldn't put it past Gran!

"The guests are starting to arrive," Gran explained. "This is Mr. Henderson's. Marsh is going to be here for the whole festival."

"Oh really?" Vivi took another look at the 'vette and wondered about the owner. Mr. Henderson was probably middle-aged and bald, trying to recapture his youth with a flashy car and a wardrobe to match. She had seen the type in St. Louis, but they seldom came to the Covered Bridge Festival.

Fifty weeks of the year, Rockville was a quiet small town near the Illinois-Indiana line. Two U.S. highways—36 and 41—crossed there, but the interstate network had robbed them of much of their previous traffic.

In October, however, when the fall foliage was at its peak the Covered Bridge Festival brought tourists— some 500,000 of them—pouring into the area from all over the country to explore the scenic rolling country-side with its attractive villages and numerous quaint covered wooden bridges.

Motels throughout the area were jammed, and local people, like Gran, rented rooms or provided bed-and-breakfast for tourists during the festival. Many tourists returned year after year, becoming friends of their hosts.

Several times since her teens Vivi had taken her vacation at this season to come stay with Gran and help with the cooking and housework. She loved Rockville, the festival, and the knowledge that she was helping her grandmother.

"My, my, you have gone citified!" Gran declared. "Look at all this fancy luggage you brought!"

"And you be careful not to scratch or dent it!" Vivi said severely before breaking up with laughter. She handed out shopping bags from department stores and Waldenbooks. Her skirts and jeans and tops were in plastic bags from the dry cleaners.

They went up the front steps and across the broad veranda to the carved oak door, through the spacious entry hall, then up the staircase which rose in graceful dignity to the second floor, and on up a narrower stair to the attic.

Vivi found herself panting and wondering at Gran's vigor. She climbed briskly without breathing hard, even with a bag in each hand.

"Here you are—your very own nest," Gran announced when they arrived at the top.

Vivi gave a loving glance around. She'd always adored the attic rooms, particularly this one at the very top of the big old house. It looked out into the trees, orange and gold in autumn. The room was circular, with several windows giving views in all directions. The wallpaper was rosebud-sprigged, and the woodwork was white-painted. The old furniture, originally sent to the attic for storage, was back in fashion—a single bed of cherry with a nightstand beside it, an armoire, and a small bureau with an oval mirror hanging above it. As a little girl, she'd played princess in this tower and daydreamed and read stories for hours on end.

"You haven't changed much," Gran commented shrewdly, dumping the Walden's bag onto the wedding-ring quilt which served as a bedspread. "Mercy! When do you expect to read all of these?"

Vivi laughed easily. "You know me! I'll read the fine print on the back of a cereal box if there's nothing better at hand," she quipped as she began to stack the colorful paperbacks on the low nightstand shelf.

A Bible was already there. Vivi eyed it askance and wondered if Gran, a pillar of her church, had started putting a Bible in each guest room, the way the Gideons did in hotels and motels?

Gran noticed the glance. "That's a new translation," she proudly informed Vivi. "I had some doubts about it when I began hearing about it, and I do miss some of the traditional phrasing, but no denying, it is easier to read and understand. Knowing how you love to read, I thought you might enjoy it while you're here."

"Oh…er…yes," Vivi dubiously agreed. The paperbacks she'd brought were more her style.

Gran patted her shoulder. "I'd better get back downstairs. The O'Haras are due to arrive anytime. Come down when you're ready, and we'll have tea and cookies."

"Molasses hermits?" Vivi questioned hopefully. They'd been her favorites from childhood, and Gran usually baked a batch whenever Vivi came. "Mmmm!" She'd inherited Gran's metabolism as well as appearance. They could eat like harvest hands yet stay model-slim, to the despair of their dieting friends.

Gran bustled back downstairs, and Vivi busied herself unpacking. The tiny tower room didn't allow any clutter; anything out of place made it seem to be a shambles. It lacked sufficient storage space, even in the nearby old-fashioned bathroom. In fact, most of these attic rooms had been servant quarters and were too small to be rented out.

Knowing the tower room's limitations, Vivi had held her packing to a minimum. Jeans, T's, and shirts would do equally well for household chores and wandering about in Rockville and Billie Creek Village, the reconstructed settlement just east of town on Route 36, and for driving to see the bridges and autumn color and festival events in the nearby towns.

She had one dress along. Gran was sure to want her to join her at church both of the Sundays she'd be here, and she might need the dress for some other occasion, as well, though she couldn't imagine what.

Vivi heaved a sigh of contentment. Oh, but it was good to be here—to be on vacation—for the next ten days! Away from the apartment she shared with Jill, away from the television station where she was a copywriter—most of all, away from all her problems.

Jill was getting married at Christmas, and she was only technically still living in the apartment now. She spent most of her free time with her fiancé, which made Vivi feel uncomfortable. Having Jill married and actually moving in with him would be a relief.

But—could Vivi find another roommate who'd be as congenial in most respects? Face it—any roommate at all would create difficulties, now that she'd had the apartment virtually to herself all this time.

And—if Vivi didn't find a roommate—what then? She couldn't afford to stay on in the apartment by herself, at least not very long.

What else could she do? She could always go back under her parents' roof. She'd left in the first place, however, because it was out in the suburbs, a long commute to work. Moreover, her parents still saw her as a little girl, in need of their protection and guidance, not a grown woman quite capable of managing on her own.

Of course there was always Barry. He was unbelievably good looking—and even more unbelievably in love with her.

Unfortunately, he was divorced, and after an extremely disagreeable marriage and painful breakup, he was leery of risking such a commitment again soon. His declarations and promises were all designed to make Vivi his live-in lover—not his wife. At any rate, not his wife right at the start. A trial relationship, he had urged persuasively just last week.

She could understand his feelings. Of course he'd have doubts and fears. The old, "Once bitten, twice shy," and "The burned child fears the fire." Only, Vivi wished he'd try harder to understand how she felt.

Was she the only remaining woman of twenty-three who wanted to be a virgin on her wedding night? Who would be mortified to have her parents—and worse yet, Gran!—know she was living with a man without being married to him?

Everyone else she knew seemed so much more sophisticated, so casual about divorce and live-in lovers, whom they seemed to change with confusing rapidity. She didn't condemn them. They could lead their lives however they pleased.

And she found Barry intensely attractive and exciting, but she wanted to be very certain that love was real, sanctified by a marriage ceremony with family and close friends present. Vivi wanted her husband to know that he had been and always would be the only man in her life.

So now she had almost two weeks to figure out how to handle her situation back home. Briefly she drifted into a delicious daydream in which Barry rushed to Rockville to take her into his arms and murmur ardently that he couldn't stand it without her, even for these few vacation days—that he wanted them to marry.

Vivi shook her head, smiling slightly. Unlikely! Barry was just as determined as she was. Sometimes she wondered whether they'd ever get together, far apart as they were about what they wanted from life.

A brisk knock on the open door made her whirl in surprise. She hadn't heard anyone coming!

A man stood there, surveying her with keen greenish-hazel eyes. His thick dark hair came so close to the top of that doorway that he had to be at least six feet tall, and his broad shoulders, in a cranberry corduroy shirt, seemed to fill it. He was—what? Thirty? Not over thirty-five, she felt certain. He had a strong face. Smile lines fanned at the outer corners of his eyes, and his mouth was straight and firm, yet conveyed gentleness. Those shoulders tapered to lean hips and long legs in casual denims, ending in large feet, well-shod in suede desert boots. That accounted for the silence of his approach.

"I didn't mean to startle you," he said matter-of-factly. Her work at the television station made her aware of voices and appearance. He had a good voice, an easy baritone, with an attractive soft southern drawl. "Your car seems to be blocking mine, and the keys aren't in it. Suppose you could move it?"

"Oh—of course—I'm sorry!" Vivi exclaimed, flustered. "I didn't realize! I was so happy to get here and see Gran. I did mean to move it, except then I got sidetracked to unpacking, and—" She gestured ruefully.

"No big deal," he reassured, and the accompanying smile crinkled his eyes. "I can shift it for you, if you'll give me the keys...?"

"Oh, no, no—I will," she said. "You're—" Her mind searched for the name Gran had said. "Mr. Henderson?"

"Marshall William Henderson," he enlarged upon it, still smiling at her as if he liked what he saw—very much. "Make it Marsh. And besides being Mrs. Gordon's granddaughter from St. Louis, you're—?"

"Vivian Louise Gordon," she supplied, smiling back at him as she started down the stairs. When she glanced up from several steps below him, he really towered above her. "My mother was a *Gone with the Wind* fan; I understand I came close to being Scarlett. Vivian Leigh played Scarlett," she added in case his memory needed jogging, "and Mother also liked Vivian Vance, Lucille Ball's sidekick on all the old 'Lucy' shows." She was babbling. Why? He must think her an absolute idiot. Echoing him, she said, "Make it Vivi. Everyone does."

"I have the rear room," he remarked, as they reached the bedroom floor. He gestured toward it. "Nice, though it doesn't have the view your aerie does."

"Neither does it have all the stairs to climb," Vivi said lightly. "Didn't Gran say you'll be here for the entire festival?"

"That's right. Combined business and pleasure. I can go to Terre Haute and Indianapolis and other towns quite easily from here."

"Yes—they're no distance at all from here." Well, Indianapolis was more than an hour's drive, but in that

14

Corvette....She wondered what his business was. Would she seem nosy if she asked? Probably. "Of course, sometimes when the festival's in full swing, the streets are such a traffic jam that it's hard to get anywhere."

"I know. That's how I got to know the festival the first time. I was making a routine run to Indianapolis, and it took half an hour to get through town, instead of the usual five minutes. The crowds fascinated me to the point that I stopped to explore. This makes three times I've stayed here. I don't think you were here the first two though." His gaze was intent, hazel eyes friendly.

"No, I wasn't. I like to come for the festival, but it isn't always possible to get vacation at the right time."

They reached the front door and went out, cutting across the lawn to their cars in the drive.

"Hmmm, we seem to have something in common," he observed, with a lurking smile. "A fondness for red!" He glanced from car to car, then to the brightness of her T-shirt. "Perhaps your mother should have named you Scarlett after all!"

Vivi laughed back up at him and slid into her car, carefully reversed, and then pulled forward to park next to his Corvette. She doubted she'd need her car before Monday, so if it got blocked, that was all right. Everywhere in Rockville was walking distance, and the two weekends of the festival were the most hectic. Next week would be time enough to go out to Billie Creek Village and on the scenic drives.

She watched, enjoying his athletic coordination as he eased into his car, ducking his head. His cranberry corduroy shirt went better with the gleaming scarlet of the car than she would have supposed.

He lifted his left hand to her in a salute of farewell and thanks as he backed down the drive. Interesting. Completely bare. No wedding ring or signet ring which might hide a ring, and no pale line left by a ring. Anyway if he were married, wouldn't he have his wife along, inasmuch as he was staying ten days or more? Maybe not.

What difference did it make, anyway? She had Barry. She loved him and he loved her. Not in the same way, precisely, but given time—oh, surely, given a little time to get over the trauma of his failed marriage. Why was she even looking at other men, interested in whether they wore wedding rings?

"Vivi!" Gran called as Vivi reentered the house. "Ready for your tea and cookies?"

"They sound perfect." Vivi followed the sound of Gran's voice to the kitchen.

If a kitchen is the heart of a house, this house had a warm heart. Counters were of a tawny wood, with orange formica tops, coppertone range and refrigerator and massive freezer, and there was a big rectangular oak table in the center of the room. The wallpaper was patterned with luscious-looking carrots. A bay window overlooked the back yard, with a round breakfast table and chairs of yellow-painted bentwood. And Gran's beloved African violets were everywhere.

"So, you met Marsh, did you?" Gran queried, pouring tea from a fat ceramic pot into matching mugs and pushing a platter of cookies nearer Vivi. "I baked these this morning."

"Yes, I had to move my—" Vivi broke off, to survey Gran with suspicion. Was that wrinkled face just a little too guileless; were the brown eyes too innocent? "Gran—if you've got any ideas about matchmaking, it's only fair to warn you, I'm practically engaged!"

"You are?" Gran's pleased surprise was followed by a puzzled frown at Vivi's slim fingers. "I don't see any engagement ring."

"Well…no—we haven't picked one out yet." Besides, the engagement wasn't formal. How could there be an engagement when Barry was obdurately opposed to remarriage and she herself had some doubts about their rightness for one another? "Anyway, I don't like diamonds. We could spend the money to better advantage in other ways. Just a nice broad gold wedding band would be enough to suit me."

Her eyes went to Gran's arthritic fingers, the worn band on the left hand. Grandpa'd placed that ring there on their wedding day, and Gran had never removed it. That had always seemed tremendously romantic and meaningful to Vivi, and she longed to emulate it.

"Tell me about your young man," Gran invited, smiling and interested. "What's he like?"

"His name's Barry. We work together at the TV station, but he's a salesman, not a copywriter. After he sells the spots, he brings me the information and I write the ads. He has fair hair and the bluest eyes, and he isn't too tall…." Vivi's voice trailed off dreamily as she visualized him, seeing the smile that made his eyes deepen and sparkle in a special look for her, hearing him lower his voice to an intimate murmur….

"I'm surprised you'd come over here for all this time, with him back there," Gran commented. "Maybe I should've talked Patti into coming?"

Vivi shook herself off. "Oh, no! I wanted to come! You know the old saying about absence making the heart grow fonder."

"Hmmm. Of somebody else, they generally go on to add," Gran said tartly. Her eyes were too sharp. "Well, be nice to Marshall Henderson anyway. He's good company, and what's the harm in knowing more than one fine man?"

"I should hope I'll be nice to everybody staying here," Vivi said with dignity. "And I think Patti is going steady with somebody."

"That Patti," Gran said, shaking her head with tolerant affection. "You like this job of yours, do you? Just what does a copywriter do?"

"Writes copy," Vivi quipped, eyes sparkling. Then she became more serious. "Well, I told you that when Barry and the other salesmen sell advertising time, they bring me all the information. Who the client is, what they specifically want to promote in the ads, and whether the ads are sixty-, thirty-, twenty-, or ten-second spots. Often it's some of each. Then it's up to me to write that up, with appropriate film or slides, to persuade viewers to rush right out and buy the product. It's challenging, particularly if it isn't for something I like myself."

Gran frowned at that. "You mean you have to sell things you don't believe in?"

"No, no," Vivi reassured. "Just—well, I like the little cars like my Fiesta, but maybe a car dealer wants to push big ones. Or an amusement park's promoting its really scary new ride. *I* don't like huge limos or thrill-seeking, but a lot of people do. And most of the ads I do are for really interesting things that I do like, such as a greenhouse or a nice restaurant."

Gran nodded, not pushing the matter. "It's nice that you're where you see your young man every day. You told me awhile back that your roommate's getting married this Christmas. Maybe the two of you can get married and move in right then?"

"Oh, no, I doubt that," Vivi said dubiously. "Not that soon. I never realized how much planning goes into a big wedding. Even a medium or small wedding, for that matter, and I'd like to have some of the trimmings."

"Yes, you don't want to just elope." Gran's expression turned nostalgic. "Your parents were married right here in this house. Your mother was such a beautiful bride, coming down those stairs in her long white gown and lace veil."

"That would be lovely," Vivi agreed, visualizing it, with herself as the bride, descending on Dad's arm, with her groom waiting in the living room, in front of the fireplace, while misty-eyed relatives and friends beamed. Shaking the vision off, she said briskly, "I'll have to find a new roommate, and that may not be easy. I don't even know where to begin looking. If I advertise, who knows what I'd get?"

Gran nodded, and sipped her tea, mulling that over. "I wonder, does your church have a bulletin board or a newsletter? You might find a nice girl that way."

"Yes…" Vivi assented, hesitating to tell Gran that she didn't attend church regularly enough to have any notion. And while she didn't want a swinger, neither did she want a strait-laced do-gooder mate who'd preach at her and disapprove of what she did and said.

"We'll think about it," Gran promised encouragingly. "I don't want to be an old busybody, telling you what to do, but I have lived a good many years. Maybe while you're here, we can come up with something. And of course, we can both pray about it."

"Yes, we can." Vivi could agree with that without

reservation. She had kept the habit of saying a quick prayer in request or thanks. Gran was right, praying for help in finding a roommate—and solving the problem with Barry—might be the right idea.

"You've got enough time," Gran reminded, and sipped the last of the tea in her cup. "All this week for us to think—and then over two months before you need that roommate. Anything can happen by then. But you start the new year right, with the right new roommate."

"A new beginning," Vivi said contemplatively. "Yes, Gran, I'll do that. I knew spending my vacation with you was the thing to do. You've already made me feel better."

She and Gran exchanged smiles of mutual affection. Gran peered at their cups and then poured more tea. As they both reached for another cookie, they heard the thud of feet out on the veranda.

"The O'Haras—at long last," Gran surmised, rising. "I've been looking for them all afternoon!"

Briskly, she hurried out to greet them. Vivi sat on at the table, gazing out the bay window at the back yard and nibbling at a fat molasses cookie. Mentally, she shared the view, the tea, and the cookies with a male companion.

To her surprise, the companion of her imagination didn't have Barry's fair crest and baby blue eyes. The hair was thick and dark, and the eyes were hazel with green flecks and had smile crinkles at the corners.

Chapter Two

"There!" Gran said with satisfaction. "We're finished for today! You can run along and enjoy yourself."

"Right now I'm going to enjoy myself taking a nice long bath," Vivi said ruefully. She stretched stiffly.

Making beds and vacuuming a house this size was no light task! Some beds had to be stripped and made up fresh as guests checked out, with sheets and pillowcases stuffed into the washer, load after load.

Fortunately, most guests stayed several days; some even made their own beds, treating this like the home of a friend, not a hotel. Marsh Henderson was one of those, and his room was very neat. He kept a few books and papers on the dresser, but left none of the clutter Vivi found in some rooms.

Gran chuckled. "Personally, I'm going to take the newspaper to my room and stretch out on the bed!" Her room was at the back of the ground floor, with its own compact bathroom. "You do as you please and don't worry about me. If you want to have lunch, go right ahead."

In keeping with the routine of previous visits, Vivi was free to sample the frontier American delicacies offered at festival booths. If she chose to come home for lunch, there were soups in the cupboard and various sandwich-makings in the refrigerator.

Vivi poured a generous blob of her favorite bath oil into the hot water as it streamed into the old-timey, claw-footed oval tub. All the other baths in the house had been modernized at least once but this one beside Vivi's tower room was untouched except for occasional fresh paint on the wainscoted walls. Fragrant steam perfumed the small room as the tub filled.

For a while she luxuriated, soaking away the weariness, but she wasn't the sort to enjoy idleness more than a short time, certainly not with so many favorite places to revisit!

Soon she was out and toweled dry. Then she pulled on clean casual clothes, brushed-denim jeans in a particularly mellow shade of blue and a blue-and-white plaid shirt with tabbed sleeves and a metallic thread, which glittered in the sunshine. An echoing glitter came from the small gold studs in her ears and the ring of Black Hills gold in a rose design on her right hand.

As she trotted down the broad staircase, Vivi called to Gran that she was leaving before she hurried on down the walk and headed toward town.

The square was only a few blocks away, and cars lined the curbs, bumper to bumper. Gran's drive was full of guests' cars, and so were those of the other houses with tourist rooms. Many more drivers cruised around, hoping against hope to find a just-vacated parking spot.

Numerous people were out on foot, all heading for the courthouse square. Footsteps crackled in the fallen leaves which spiraled down from trees to drift on sidewalks and in gutters.

Vivi loved this town, with its quaint old homes so lovingly tended and newer homes of all sizes and styles. She loved it during its usual sleepy quiet and enjoyed its hectic bustle during the fall festival and the maple-sugaring activities in mid-winter. The "First Saturday" markets, held from May through October, were comparatively new, but she'd heard they were beginning to draw good crowds, too.

What a pity Barry couldn't come with her! He'd enjoy this—wouldn't he? He liked discos and lively, sophisticated entertainments, but those just happened to be the places they had gone together. Six Flags and a rock concert and the Muny, the Municipal Opera. He would like this, too. Of course he would.

How she'd revel in introducing him to Gran and then showing him around town. Vivi grinned at the reluctant thought that it was just as well that he hadn't come along. Where would he sleep?

There wasn't a room to be had anywhere in town; most places had been booked up weeks and even months ahead. Even if they were married, he couldn't share her tower room; the bed was too narrow.

"Cinderella off to the ball?" A masculine voice with a trace of southern drawl spoke in her ear.

Vivi jumped and turned, startled. "You are the quietest-walking man I've ever known!" she declared, both amused and vexed at Marsh's second approach. "Can't you clomp a little bit?"

He grinned back, though he didn't look particularly penitent. "Sorry about that! Finished your chores?"

"Finally," she conceded, "although I can't see Gran as a wicked stepmother—and I don't have a pumpkin coach or a coachman or a ball gown, either."

"Wrong time of day for ball gowns," he said gravely,

23

shaking his head, "and this traffic would frighten the horses."

"Oh—right," she agreed, slanting a smile up at him. A breeze gave her a whiff of his aftershave, subtle and spicy and very nice—very nice indeed. It seemed particularly appropriate for autumn, blending well with the smoke where fallen leaves had been raked and burned.

Companionably they walked together the rest of the way to the square, passing the library and a pleasant old church and smiling at the welcoming message on its notice board out front. He must have been walking faster, since he'd overtaken her, but now he seemed content to match his strides to hers.

The massive old courthouse was virtually hidden by all the crowds around it. A huge tent, full of craft exhibit booths, extended around half of it. Smaller tents and log lean-tos were all along the other half, with six black iron cauldrons of ham and beans simmering over open fires on the west side. On the opposite side of the square, long charcoal grills were ready to barbecue tonight's dinner—chicken, ribs, perhaps both. Vivi felt a thrill of hungry anticipation, remembering from past years how delicious that would be.

Big yellow school buses lined the west side of the square to take tourists on sightseeing tours of the four scenic routes to view the county's thirty-four covered bridges and the colorful autumn foliage of the rolling countryside.

So many things to see! For a while she and Marsh wandered along together, looking at the log lean-to offering country-cured hams and whole sides of bacon, and others selling sandwiches of sausage or country ham on homemade bread. Yet another had homemade ice cream, persimmon or vanilla. Crullers were deep-fried and sugared, their aroma combining temptingly with that of coffee from the big urn on the counter.

In the craft tent, Vivi and Marsh were separated. That was just as well. His companionship was pleasant, but she wasn't hunting for romance. She already had Barry.

On Saturday morning, this tent was really packed with fascinated tourists, browsing and buying. Ceramics of every sort were offered, and hand-tooled leather goods. Notepaper and postcards depicted many of the local covered bridges. Quilted items. Knits and crochets. Macramé. Potted plants. Gourds, pumpkins, and squash. Old-fashioned wooden toys. Dried-flower arrangements. Paperweights. Hand-dipped candles. Tole-painted items. The variety was really amazing.

Fudge, homemade breads and cakes and cookies, jams and jellies. As always, Vivi was surprised at what could be flavored with persimmons and pawpaws and corncobs! Actually, she found the corncob jelly and candy tasteless, just rosy and anonymously sweet, but it seemed very popular. Maple sugar was used in numerous ways, too, and molded into fancy shapes.

At the information booth outside, she picked up a copy of the Covered Bridge Festival newspaper and a map, and when she went back inside the big tent, she bought some pumpkin cookies, then scolded herself. With Gran's molasses hermits filling the cookie jar at home, why buy more cookies here? At another booth, she got a plastic shopping bag with a covered bridge depicted on the side—luggage for the trip home!—and put the papers and cookies in that.

She browsed on, admiring some clever soft-

how many people were talented at creating this sort of thing! Her only flair was for using words. It made her a good copywriter, but it would be nice to do crafts, too.

She saw Marsh Henderson again when she went inside the courthouse to study the art exhibit paintings on the corridor walls.

"Been busy shopping?" he greeted her, eyeing the bag hung over her arm.

She shook her head, brown eyes sparkling. "Not yet! So far I'm just looking." The cookies hardly counted. "Hmm. Do these sheep look like any you've ever seen?" she asked, critically studying a watercolor.

He shrugged. "For all I know about sheep! That landscape has nice balance and color."

They wandered together, examining and discussing the various paintings, though Vivi was careful—and suspected he was, too—not to say anything critical; often the artists were around, watchful and proud, and she didn't want to hurt anyone's feelings. Some paintings were extremely good, while others suffered by comparison. A few she loved; others might be technically superior but were less appealing to her. Most, quite naturally, were autumn landscapes of the surrounding hills, with a covered bridge prominently featured. They probably sold best to tourists wanting a remembrance of the festival.

Her appetite stirred as they went out the west door of the courthouse. The aromas of spicy doughnuts, coffee, woodsmoke, and the ham-and-bean dinners vied with one another. Vivi sniffed hungrily and glanced at her neat, small digital watch. To her surprise it was past noon.

26

"High time," Marsh agreed. "Ham and beans? I'll buy."

"Yes, but Dutch," she specified, tone pleasant but firm, as they joined the line of other hungry festival-goers.

He inspected her with interest. "Feminist?"

"Engaged," she said crisply. "Barry isn't the jealous type, but I don't think he'd like somebody else buying lunch for me." She got out her money as they neared the serving counter where women swiftly filled orders.

"You aren't wearing any ring," he said, as Gran had. "On the finger that counts, that is."

"I don't need a ring to be committed," she informed him. "The wedding ring will be enough, when that time comes. Until then, as long as I'm going with Barry—" She broke off as she reached the counter. She accepted her bowl of ham and beans, paid for it, and moved on toward the condiment table.

He shook his head, as he followed her. "Now if I were engaged to a woman like you, I'd want a ring on her to warn other men away!"

"Onions?"

Vivi blinked at the incongruity of the question. Then she smiled back at a man helping with the condiments. "Yes, please," she said, and watched him spoon chopped onion onto her plate of cornbread, beans, and ham.

"Not planning on kissing anybody, then?" the man teased.

"Nobody who hasn't also eaten onions," Marsh joked back. He gave a nod to the spoon hovering over the onions. "Same for me, thanks."

Vivi led the way to a comparatively empty picnic table, feeling nettled. What right did he have to quiz her about whether she wore a ring and to allow that man to think he planned to kiss her? Then she shook it off. No right, obviously, but it wasn't worth dignifying by letting it annoy her.

As Marsh joined her, a family of four took most of the other seats at the table. Before they began to eat, the father quietly but distinctly said grace.

Vivi waited until he finished before she began to eat, feeling faintly like a heathen, although she didn't know why she should. She was a good person—no saint, but average-good. She tried to live by the Golden Rule and the Ten Commandments.

She shrugged that off as well. Nothing was going to annoy her today!

Eating with him, Vivi became conscious of Marsh's hands—long and strong and tanned, with well-tended nails. He used his hands with a deft economy of movement. Beans and shredded onion weren't the easiest of foods to eat—she knew all too well!—but he didn't seem to have trouble managing his. She hadn't noticed a single bean dropping down onto his lap or plate. He must think she was a slob.

"For dessert we could go have persimmon ice cream," he suggested, as their plates emptied.

She considered, then smiled at him. "That would be good. I wonder if it's really homemade?"

It was. She couldn't detect much flavor, but maybe the raw onions had dulled her palate for more delicate tastes. Strolling in the early afternoon sun eating ice cream was pleasant, peaceful. There was a lot to be said for old-time pastimes.

Attention on her ice cream, she didn't particularly watch where she was going. Suddenly her toe caught.

She pitched forward, grabbing—but there was nothing but air to grab as she floundered for balance.

Muscular arms clamped about her waist, checking her fall and pulling her against a long, hard body. Her face was buried against Marsh's shirt, a fine dark wool plaid today. The sound of his heart rhythmically thudding against her cheek and ear seemed to spread throughout her entire body. His aftershave scent filled her nostrils as she gasped.

He stared down into her eyes for a second which seemed an eternity, their faces so close that she could distinctly see the dilation of his pupils and the gleaming flecks of green, gold, and brown in the hazel irises.

For a moment he held her close, and she clung to him. Then she pulled away slightly, and he released her, his hands sliding to her waist, steadying her.

She'd never been so close to a man except when he was going to kiss her, and involuntarily her gaze fell to his lips—firmly sculpted, wide and lean, sensual yet sensitive—and she wondered, *How would they feel?*

Faintly shocked at herself, Vivi stiffened and stepped back, hoping she wasn't coloring but afraid she was. Barry! Think of Barry, back home in St. Louis waiting for her, in love with her—

"Hey," Marsh said softly, an undercurrent of amusement in his voice, "it's a good thing we both ate onions, isn't it? And look at you—you didn't even drop your ice cream!"

"Oh, I'm very careful not to waste any food," Vivi said at random.

"As a little girl, did your mother remind you of the starving Third World countries and enroll you in the Clean Plate Club?" he queried with lively interest.

"And she made me eat my carrots," Vivi gravely

confirmed. "I *liked* spinach and broccoli."

"You didn't! You were a disgrace to childhood!" His eyes glinted down at her.

"Yes…well…what can I say?" she appealed, wide-eyed.

They wandered about the square together for a while, before going back into the long tent to look again at the craft items. Every time Vivi went through, she noticed something different. They called one another's attention to ridiculously inappropriate items. What on earth would he want with a lamp which had a hoopskirted doll as a base? What would she do with a yard-long green calico snake?

Eventually the press of the crowd separated them. Vivi felt a sense of relief. She didn't want to spend the entire day with the man, however pleasant he was! But she peered about for him anyway. His height should make him easy to find. Unfortunately, her petite size limited her view, and she seemed surrounded by extra-large people.

With a shrug, she gave it up, and when she reached an exit, she decided she'd had enough festival for one day. She really ought to go home and see whether Gran needed her. Or maybe Gran would enjoy coming to the square for a while, to see what booths were new from last year and to speak to her friends who were working there.

Progress was slow along the crowded sidewalks. Vivi was relieved when she finally saw Gran's big white house up ahead. She admired it with affection. After many years of being considered architectural monstrosities, Victorian houses were back in favor, and this one was a fine example, with its tower and gables and verandas and frosty wooden-lace trim.

The lawn spread around it like a green velvet skirt decorated with carefully tended flowerbeds. A double garage was behind the house. Gordons had lived here for a hundred years, and in other homes in Parke County before building this mansion.

Approaching it, Vivi saw the scarlet Corvette parked in the driveway, brilliantly gleaming in the afternoon sun. It reminded her of its owner—the firmness of his hands on her waist, the thump of his heart against her ear, the scent of his aftershave. He smelled so clean and masculine and good. What kind of cologne was that?

"I'll take a look, next time I clean his room," she said under her breath. Barry should like that fragrance. She could get him some for Christmas which was really only a few weeks away. That solved a problem, for she was always puzzled about what to buy for men. She smiled, thinking this would be a gift for herself, as well. She'd appreciate a male who smelled so masculinely delicious!

Gran was sitting on the porch in the wooden swing, enjoying the fine warm afternoon weather. Vivi perched on the top step, back against the column, relaxed and companionable.

"Mercy, no, I've seen my fill of festivals," Gran replied to Vivi's suggestion. "I can do without all that crowd, at my age. You're my little lamb to think of it, though. Did you have a good time? What did you have for lunch? Did you see Marsh Henderson there?"

"We had ham and beans together," Vivi told her. "And onions." Her lips curved in an involuntary smile at the memories which onions evoked.

"You won't want much supper, then," Gran surmised, eyes twinkling.

31

"Well—" Vivi threw a sparkling glance up at her. "By that time I imagine I could manage to eat something! What do you have in mind? Or shall I fix something?"

"You might make your 'macaroni mess' sometime while you're here," Gran replied. "I've got everything you'd need for it on hand, I think."

"I'll go check," Vivi offered, jumping up. "Tonight?"

If any ingredients were lacking, she'd have ample time to walk to the grocery. However, Gran's freezer and cupboards and pantry were always so well stocked that Vivi considered any lack unlikely.

The "macaroni mess" looked, smelled, and tasted far better than its undignified name indicated. As she found one ingredient after another, Vivi decided she might as well begin preparing it. It tasted better if it sat for a while after cooking. First she sautéed the uncooked seashell macaroni, then added tomato sauce, chopped onion and garlic, Italian herbs and green pepper. Then she turned the burner down so the "mess" could simmer gently for an hour.

Vivi trotted briskly up the steep, narrow back stairs, up and up till she reached her tower aerie, and grabbed one of the paperback romances from the bedside table, and returned to the kitchen. She could read between trips to stir the macaroni.

The story was lively and entertaining. The hero and heroine went to bed together early in the story with the knowledge and apparently full approval of all the heroine's family and friends. Maybe Barry was right. Still—Vivi couldn't imagine her parents, much less Gran, beaming and joking so approvingly under such circumstances. Moreover, the women she knew who did fall madly in love and move in with a boyfriend never seemed to find much happiness. Euphoria at the start, progressing to mutual criticism, scraps, and all too soon they'd split up, full of angry recriminations. How often had friends cried on her shoulder? Better to have loved and lost—but was that really love? *Really* love? Really *love*?

She laid down the slim volume and got up, crossing to uncover the pasta and stir. It was starting to cook down nicely, but it still had a while to go. Returning to her chair and book, Vivi shrugged off her doubts. *Suspension of disbelief* was necessary with any sort of fiction, printed or filmed. When well done, the story so caught up the reader or viewer that it all seemed entirely natural and believable. Perhaps she had read too many romances and was getting overly critical!

Instead of sitting down with her book again, Vivi wandered over to inspect the freezer and refrigerator, to see what she could fix to go with the macaroni. Salad. Gran had plenty of carrots and lettuce, and she could chop up the rest of the green pepper. Now, what vegetable? As if in replay, she heard herself telling Marsh, "*I LIKE spinach*," and she reached to take a package of frozen spinach from the freezer, opening it and putting it on the countertop to start thawing.

"Now this is what I like, somebody who takes over the cooking," Gran commented, coming in and sociably sitting down at the bay-window table. "I get mighty tired of my own food!"

"Gran! You're a wonderful cook!" Vivi protested. Her mother had always said it was a talent as hereditary as Gran's brown eyes and curly hair.

"That's as may be, but by the time you reach my age, you'll know what I mean," Gran predicted. "A change is welcome. Sometimes I think I'd eat anything, long's I don't have to cook it."

"I'll give you a vacation, then, while I'm here." Vivi enjoyed having a big spacious kitchen, after her apartment's tiny kitchenette.

They talked of small everyday matters as Vivi watched and stirred the thickening macaroni. They discussed which guests had already arrived, who was still expected, whether to allow Kitticat the run of the house. People either loved or hated cats, and some people had allergies. Kitticat's own feelings combined outrage at being shut out of her very own domain, with not really liking so many strangers around.

"Mmmm! Something smells powerful good in here!" Marsh sauntered in from the hall with Kitticat in his arms. He carried the tiger-striped cat like a baby; she lay relaxed on her back in his arms, and with one large gentle hand he rubbed the cat's tawny soft tummy.

"Vivi's my new cook," Gran informed him. "It's as good as it smells. Should be! I taught her everything she knows and most of what I know!" Her eyes twinkled.

"Except this recipe," Vivi amended. "I keep trying to teach it to her, but she'd rather wait and have me fix it for her."

"My ma didn't raise a fool," Gran declared smugly.

Marsh moved closer to peer into the pan as Vivi stirred. He inhaled pleasurably. "A woman after my own heart, one who likes raw onions and garlic! You brought her up right, Mrs. G."

"Stay and eat with us," Gran invited hospitably. "There's plenty."

He glanced inquiringly at Vivi before consenting.

"Yes, otherwise we'll be eating it the rest of the week," she seconded the invitation. She wasn't overly enthusiastic. Was Marsh Henderson going to be everywhere she went, doing everything she did, the whole time she was here? "But do you share my childhood fondness for spinach? That's the vegetable I've got thawing," she warned.

"I'll force myself," he promised, grinning broadly. He went over to the comfortable old basket chair and sat down, still holding Kitticat, his long legs stretched out in front of him.

"Now, we can have more than one vegetable," Gran scolded hospitably, rising and bustling over to peer into the freezer. "What's your favorite, Marsh? We've got corn—peas—green beans—limas—?"

Vivi's glance at him was half deprecating as she met his eyes, full of affectionate amusement. Their eyes locked; she couldn't look away to save her life. His eyes told her that he enjoyed Gran, valued her motherly fussing, appreciated Vivi herself coming to help out. Vivi's answered that she loved and respected her grandmother, took pleasure in her company, and appreciated his attitude.

Unwillingly, she acknowledged an intruding thought—how would Barry fit into this kitchen? What would he think of Gran—and she of him?

35

Chapter Three

"Who gets the happy-face pancakes?" Vivi questioned, balancing the full tray. She smiled down at redheaded, five-year-old Nicky O'Hara, and guessed, "This big boy?"

"No, this big boy," Mrs. O'Hara said, mock-disapprovingly, gesturing at her equally redheaded six-foot husband. "Nicky gets the eggs and sausage links."

"Well, I *like* happy-face pancakes," Mr. O'Hara defended himself, "and Mrs. Gordon knows just how to make them."

Early morning chatter surrounded Gran's dining table on Sunday.

"Hey, I never knew Mrs. G. could do neat things like that!" Marsh complained. "And I've been making do with scrambled eggs and bacon!"

"Tomorrow," Vivi promised him. "Tomorrow!"

A big, hearty breakfast was included with the room at Gran's, and it was served family style in the spacious dining room. Mother, who did calligraphy, had lettered several attractive menu cards listing choices available—tomato or orange juice, scrambled or fried eggs, bacon or sausage links, hot or cold cereal, coffee or tea or milk, buttered toast with jam or jelly or honey. It was the only meal provided, except when a favored guest was invited to share dinner with Gran, as Marsh had been last night.

As Vivi filled the now-empty tray with dishes from guests who had finished eating and carried the tray to the kitchen, she remembered their meal together the night before. Gran had asked Marsh to say grace, and he had surprised Vivi by doing so quite promptly and naturally. He was not a bit self-conscious or faltering about it.

Vivi hadn't anticipated that. It seemed incongruous from a man his age who drove a scarlet sports car! Her own mind tended to go blank at such moments, and she was relieved that the honor usually went to a man or an older person. He had made it seem entirely right to thank the Lord for good food and good company.

And, after grace, they'd fallen on the food, eating with hearty appetites which were extremely complimentary to her cooking. With Vivi's macaroni and garlic bread, they ate spinach with crumbled bacon and the buttered sweet corn Gran had insisted upon adding to the menu. Ice cream finished the meal; Gran had a passion for ice cream, especially mint chocolate chip.

Afterward they'd watched television, laughing together at a comedy. At times Vivi wondered if Marsh could possibly be enjoying the quiet family evening as much as he seemed. Or was he playing a charade, laughing at them more than the show? He seemed absolutely sincere.

Vivi's reverie was broken as Gran came into the living room to smile at all the guests and accept compliments on her cooking. "Any of you who plan on church attendance, there's a sign in the hall giving the times of services. Churches are mostly within walking distance, and anybody who wants to go with Vivi and me, you'd be most welcome," she invited hospitably.

Several people expressed interest. Church on Sunday in a small midwestern town seemed an extremely appropriate activity, though Vivi knew many would rather go on a drive to admire the autumn scenery. She wasn't sure what she'd choose, if not for Gran.

"I'd like to go with you," Marsh spoke up unhesitatingly. "I enjoyed it very much last year."

Gran beamed at him and then added for everyone in general, "It's a five-minute walk, and I like to get there a little before services start. We'll meet down here in the living room."

Getting to the church on time meant that Vivi and Gran had to push the everyday housework, washing and drying dishes, changing those beds which required it, then hurriedly showering and changing. However, they were both brisk and had worked out an efficient routine. A few less essential details could be skimmed over or skipped altogether for one day.

As Vivi pulled her soft rose wool jersey dress out of the closet, she admired its graceful draping skirt. The color was good with her gleaming short dark hair and brown eyes, and when she finished dressing, she touched her lips with gloss of the same rosy shade.

"My, don't you look nice!" Gran complimented when Vivi came downstairs. Gran herself was quite elegant, small and so straight, her navy silk dress with white polka-dots set off with a big soft bow at the throat and a little hat cocked at a jaunty angle. Marsh stood beside her.

"Two very lovely ladies," he said gallantly, a glow of

admiration lighting his eyes as he surveyed Vivi.

She sparkled back at him, thinking that he looked absolutely gorgeous himself. He'd looked good in his slacks and tartan wool shirts, but he was magnificent in this coffee-brown suit! It was beautifully tailored, emphasizing the broadness of his shoulders, his lean hips and long legs. Vivi liked a vest on a man, and his shirt was snowy white, with gold links on the French cuffs and a matching gold tie tack on what looked like an Italian silk tie in a small muted pattern. He obviously shopped in good stores.

Adding his clothes up with his expensive sports car, Vivi wondered for the first time, what Marsh did for a living. Whatever it was, he was obviously successful at it.

Several other people joined them by the time they started to church. This, Vivi realized, was fun! The group of them strolled along past the square on this splendid Sunday morning. The October air was sharp and dry, yet with a magnificent bouquet, clear and still so they weren't all windblown by the time they reached the church.

Gran had scheduled departure and arrival times nicely. With her in the lead to set the pace, they arrived with just a pleasant interval to settle in pews and listen to the organ before services began.

Vivi found herself between Gran and Marsh in a pew in the middle of the church. She gazed about, saying a silent hello to the stained-glass window above the dignified pulpit of dark wood. She'd always enjoyed accompanying Gran to this lovely old church. Admiring the window's hues of sapphire, ruby, emerald, topaz, and amethyst, she wished Gran's house had just one stained-glass window, as so many Victorian mansions did.

Why had she drifted away from the timelessly comforting quality of church services? Throughout childhood she'd always gone. High school, too. But with college and then working...Peer pressure?

With a flash of perception, Vivi wondered how many of the other girls in the dorm had felt precisely as she had, wanting to go, feeling a little guilty for abstaining, yet doing what everyone else did? Perhaps if one strong character had announced, "I'm going to church," the whole group would have gone along, relieved and happy. She could have been that strong one.

She was going to change things. When she returned to St. Louis, she was going to quietly resume attending church. Her roommate certainly wouldn't make her self-conscious. Heavens, Jill was hardly there, especially on weekends! The same with Barry. On his days off, he slept late. He wouldn't be around to tease her about "getting religion."

The minister's deep, flexible voice signaled the beginning of the service. The congregation was large, increased by tourists, and all joined in singing hymns Vivi remembered from childhood. She shared a book with Marsh. Standing so close to him she was aware of the subtle spiciness of his aftershave again and of his lean bronzed fingers on the hymnal. His singing voice was mellow and assured.

Her mind wandered as the minister made announcements of parish events. In a fleeting daydream, this wasn't Marsh but Barry, singing and worshiping next to her. Would he? She'd invite him to go with her.

Back home, changing to a casual blouse and denim

skirt before lunch, Vivi wondered whether the services had carried her away. Hadn't she made such glowing mental resolutions before, staying with Gran, only to have them wilt and fade away upon her return to ordinary routines?

Vivi half expected Marsh to join them for the cold lunch Gran set out, but he was nowhere to be seen. His car was still in the drive, wedged in behind several others, so he had to be somewhere in Rockville, on foot. Or possibly he was on one of the sightseeing bus tours of the covered bridge routes.

Only in mid-afternoon, when she was out on the veranda, writing a quick postcard note to her parents, and a longer note to Barry, did Marsh stride up the front walk, his step quickening when he saw her curled up on the old-fashioned porch swing. His suit coat was hooked over his shoulder by one finger, and he still looked elegant.

He dropped down onto the other end of the swing, steadying it when it bounced and maintaining a regular rhythm with easy pushes. "These old houses," he commented. "The new ones can't equal them, can they?"

"My apartment building can't," Vivi concurred. "It's one of those ordinary square brick ones, not old enough to have any character, but not new enough to be really modern or luxurious—although on my salary, I can't afford luxury."

"Your grandmother says you work at a TV station," he remarked conversationally. "You like that? What do you do there?"

"Yes, I do. I write advertising in the continuity department. It's a lively place, something always going on. Creative people are generally distinct individuals,

41

exciting to be around. And, of course, there's the occasional celebrity who comes in for an interview or talk show. I don't have any real contact with them, but it's still interesting to see them in person."

"Sometimes disillusioning?" Marsh suggested.

"Well...yes. If it's a star who plays a really nice person and he or she comes in whining and critical..." The image of one who'd been too drunk to be on the talk show ran quickly through Vivi's mind, but mentioning that inevitably led to questions, and Vivi didn't mean to go into that. "But for the most part, they're so attractive and full of personality, it's easy to see how they became celebrities."

"A little larger than life?" he offered, as if he, too, had met some. "You like to write? Your grandmother says you love to read. Do you have ambitions to be an author?"

Vivi shrugged, not too comfortable at being the focus of his questions and intent gaze. "Oh, like everyone who reads, of course there've been times I've finished a book and thought, *I could write one better than that*. However, I'll stick with writing advertising spots, at least for now. What about you?" She turned the conversational spotlight on him. "Do you live in an old house or just appreciate them?"

"I lived in dorms and apartment houses which must have been out of the same mold as yours, but when I moved to Paducah, I hunted and found a big old house which was divided into apartments. It isn't the house that this one is, but they have features in common. I have half the second floor; it's bigger than I really need, but I like the high ceilings and thick walls. No tower—it's steamboat Gothic—but it has a great balcony clear across the front."

42

"Oh, that sounds nice," Vivi commented. "Steamboat Gothic—that's sort of southern colonial Greek revival, isn't it?"

"Yes, a fancy one," he agreed. "Gingerbread trim and stained-glass windows and so on. Is that the kind you and the boyfriend will live in when you get married?"

"We really haven't discussed it," Vivi said guardedly. She was suddenly struck with how many subjects she avoided discussing with Barry and with the fact that she knew more of Marsh Henderson's tastes in architecture than she did Barry's.

Hurrying on to deflect further discussion, she said, "I've always loved coming to visit Gran. This house has so many nooks and crannies. My cousins and I used to have marvelous games of hide-and-seek here when the clan gathered on holidays and special occasions."

"She loves having you come visit," Marsh quietly stated. "I think you're her favorite grandchild." His warm glance intensified the compliment, implying she was a favorite of his, too. Favorite? When they'd met only day before yesterday?

Vivi shrugged, faintly embarrassed and not too sure she appreciated his flattery. She thought she'd made it clear to him that she was interested in another man and therefore not in him. Although if she didn't have Barry, she might be…receptive. Marsh was attractive, in both appearance and personality.

"Oh, each of Gran's children and grandchildren is her favorite, in one way or another," she dismissed it.

"Mmmm." He didn't look or sound convinced. "It takes a special person, I'd say, to give up a vacation to come change beds and vacuum and launder and cook

43

and wait tables and wash up afterward."

"Give up a vacation!" Vivi said indignantly. "I'm not giving up a vacation! I'm having one! I love getting in on all the festival activities. And I don't have any big hotel or restaurant bills to pay."

"Some people," he said deliberately, "would prefer to pay and not do any work."

Vivi glared at him, her brown eyes indignant. Was this developing into the same kind of teasing some of her more sophisticated friends and co-workers gave her about what they considered her square ways? He could just save it!

"Hey," he said, amused. "Hey! That's a compliment, lady! Quit bristling."

Vivi smiled ruefully. "Well, on occasion I have been called Goody-Two-Shoes."

"So who hasn't been called names sometimes?" he said philosophically. "The thing to do is to consider the source and the real meaning of an insult. From some people, the insult's better than a compliment, and some compliments are insulting."

Vivi studied him curiously. "Do you know, I never considered it that way! You do have a point there." Her eyes sparkled. "You just said you were complimenting me. Should I take that one as an insult?"

He grinned back. "No, that's a real one!" It was his turn to study Vivi. "I know your grandmother's a practicing Christian. Are you, too?"

She looked at him questioningly, unsure just how to answer.

"I noticed a Bible by your bed when I came up to ask you to move your car," he continued.

"Did you notice the stack of paperbacks, too?" Vivi queried. "I'm a compulsive reader. Anything and ev-

44

erything. Gran's got a new Bible translation and thought I might enjoy it."

"And do you?" He seemed keenly interested in the subject, waiting intently for her to reply.

She shrugged uneasily but made her tone light. "I'm still on the paperbacks. I may try it to see what people have been talking about." He was still waiting, as if expecting her to add more, so she told him, "I try to be a good person, but no, I don't get to church very often between visits here. Do you?" Let him be on the answering end, for a change.

To her surprise, he nodded. "Yes, I do. I believe in worshiping regularly with others. There are enough people who will talk about new morality and tell you everybody does this or that. It's reassuring to attend church and discover that not everybody does do those things."

Vivi stared at him in considerable astonishment. "Well—yes—it's very nice, of course, but church isn't actually necessary, is it? I mean, people can feel just as uplifted seeing beautiful scenery." She gestured in the direction of the surrounding countryside. "Not all good people go to church, and not all churchgoers are good people."

"True," he conceded, "but give the churchgoers credit for trying. There are sinners and hypocrites in any congregation but without faith and church on Sundays, there would be a lot more. We're all human, after all."

"Very human," Vivi agreed, with a small smile, not quite trusting his sincerity.

Unspoken between them from the very first was the mutual knowledge that she surprised him, interested him. He desired her. Virginity and naivete' were not synonymous. Vivi was sophisticated enough to know quite well that a man challenged by an elusive woman might do or say things he didn't really mean in order to win her over.

Had Marsh added up her grandmother's faith, the Bible in her room, and her spending her vacation here helping Gran to think she was some sort of do-gooder who could be won by a religious approach, by an appearance of being a dedicated Christian?

His next move seemed to confirm her suspicions. He reached to take her hand, to play with her slim fingers, interlacing them with his.

"I have trouble believing you're engaged, when that finger's bare," he murmured, an intimate note in his low voice, his thumb making small circles on the sensitive skin of her wrist between palm and watch band. "But I'm glad it is. That's something I don't want to believe."

"Believe it," Vivi said dryly, pulling her hand free from his big one and that too-enjoyable caress.

He shook his head. "No...as long as you aren't married or even wearing an engagement ring and you're taking a vacation clear away from where he is, I'm not giving up hope." His gaze was very direct, holding hers.

By an effort, she broke it, shaking her head and laughing. "Hope! For what? A week from now the festival will be over. You'll be going home—to Paducah, did you say? So will I, to St. Louis. And if you think I'm the sort of woman who goes in for quick holiday romances, you can think again!"

Slowly, he shook his own head in a move echoing hers. "Oh no, I don't think that, Vivi. The festival may end and we may go our separate ways, but that doesn't mean we'll never meet again. Not with cars and planes—not to mention telephones—to keep in touch between meetings."

"Well…" Vivi conceded.

If men liked to pursue women they found desirable, what woman didn't appreciate the knowledge that an attractive man found her desirable enough to pursue? It was very flattering. Also, if Barry discovered another man was in determined pursuit, he might feel differently about putting an engagement ring on her finger.

The shrill of the telephone came as a welcome interruption. Vivi was quick to jump up and hurry inside to answer it, taking along her postcards, letter, and writing materials—and a glimpse of Marsh's lazy grin.

What was he grinning about? If he thought he was winning her over or that she was running away from him, he was mistaken.

Fairly predictably, during festival week, the call was from someone who'd stayed here before and wanted to return, and she had to tell them all the rooms were reserved for the entire week.

At least this caller was one of the nice ones, complimentary about a past visit and hoping that by some miracle there'd be a vacancy.

Concentrating on the conversation, Vivi sensed Marsh had followed her in and that he stood watching and listening. She turned slightly, putting her back to him, refusing to allow him to distract her. He gave up.

He passed her where she stood near the foot of the stairs, and she felt the vibration of his quiet footfalls on the hall carpet, inhaled the faint spicy scent.

He climbed the steps until his feet were level with her eyes. She saw the small red plastic spaceship on the stair just before he stepped on it.

47

As it zoomed through the air, Marsh roared with dismay and pain.

A crash and thud made a horrendous racket in the stillness of the old house.

Vivi whirled to find Marsh sprawled at the foot of the stairs—unconscious.

Chapter Four

"You were felled by a hostile alien spacecraft?" The stocky, balding doctor surveyed Marsh quizzically. "You must have hit your head harder than I thought, young man."

"No, here it is." Vivi held up the toy, wondering whether small-town doctors still made routine calls or if this was a special favor because the doctor and Gran were neighbors and old friends.

She winced at the all-too-clear memory of how Marsh had looked, crumpled and unconscious at her feet. What a relief when he had moved and moaned almost immediately, regaining consciousness. Then, after a moment, he'd been able to get up and hobble into the living room with her help. Wincing and giving an involuntary gasp of pain, he had stretched out on the sofa.

"I should've watched where I was going, instead of looking at Vivi," Marsh said ruefully. "My own fault."

"Another time you'll know better," the doctor said tolerantly, then looked Vivi over. "Or maybe you won't. The stairs aren't as easy on the eye as she is. However, you'll have time to think it over. You won't be walking on that ankle the next few days." He glanced at Gran. "Do you still have those crutches? Better hunt them up and dust them off."

"They're up in the attic," Gran said immediately. "Vivi, you can take a look for them next time you go upstairs." Then she frowned worriedly at Marsh. "You'll have a time managing those stairs on crutches!"

He grimaced. "You mean if I can't do it with two good legs, how can I maneuver them this way?"

Vivi had a sudden, all-too-vivid mental picture of his getting tangled in the crutches and crashing down the stairs again.

Apparently Gran did, too. "You'd better trade rooms with me," she announced decisively. "I'll move upstairs to yours, and you can have my bedroom down here. It's got an adjoining bathroom, so you'll have things nice and easy."

"Good idea," the doctor confirmed. "Avoid putting weight on the ankle, and take it easy in general the rest of today, at least. You've got a mild concussion there, but rest and aspirin should help both that and the way your ankle feels."

Marsh nodded soberly and grimaced again at the way moving his head made him feel. "I should hope so."

Vivi went to the kitchen for a glass of water and the aspirin bottle Gran kept in a little first aid kit above the sink.

She felt slightly skeptical of Marsh's cooperativeness. Most men she knew considered it imperative to prove their stoic masculinity by ignoring pain. "Playing through pain," sportscasters said admiringly of athletes who ignored pulled ligaments and other injuries to compete. *Utter stupidity*, she thought but no worse than the other kind of man, who thought any minor injury or illness was life-threatening and turned into a big baby! Was Marsh going to be this kind? He certainly wasn't the first.

The doctor left, and Vivi and Gran bustled about purposefully. Gran got a laundry basket and piled into it the belongings she wanted to move upstairs. She gathered cartons to hold the contents of some of her dresser and bureau drawers so Marsh could have storage space in those.

Vivi hurried up to the attic to search out the old crutches. As she recalled, they dated back to when Grandpa broke his hip, which was also the time that the ground-floor bedroom and bath had been added to the house.

Grandpa had been a big man—maybe that was why Gran viewed Marsh so favorably—so these crutches should fit Marsh quite well. They were dusty, but wiping them off with a damp cloth took care of that and restored their luster.

Most of the job of moving Marsh's things downstairs and Gran's upstairs fell to Vivi. She repacked his suitcase and took the opportunity to make mental note of the sort of aftershave he used. This was very intimate, somehow, handling his personal things. It felt odd to be packing a man's toiletries and razor and underwear.

She glanced at his closed attaché case but resisted the temptation to look inside. Looking at the things she packed was one thing, but opening his attaché case would be snooping.

That was only the first part of it, she discovered. There was even more intimacy in unpacking for him, for he had hobbled into Gran's bedroom—now his

51

room—and stretched out on the bed.

He watched her as she unpacked, hanging his clothes in the closet or putting them in the bureau and dresser drawers. She set his toiletries and brushes out on the dresser and in the bathroom. His eyes followed her as she moved about, bending and reaching, and made her acutely self-conscious.

"You'll make some man a good wife," he commented lazily. "Coming to his rescue when he's injured, tending to his needs—all very promptly and efficiently, too. Does this what's-his-name who hasn't given you an engagement ring realize how fortunate he is?"

"Barry knows me," she smiled. "He knows a ring wouldn't make me any more his. There...I think that's everything. Do you need anything else before I go see how Gran's doing?"

"That's right, change the subject," he said tolerantly. "No. Matter of fact, whatever the doctor gave me is making me sleepy. I'll take a nap."

"That'll make you feel better," Vivi agreed. She lowered the shades to dim the impact of the bright afternoon sun, then closed the door as she left the room. She crossed to the panel window beside the front door and stood looking at the shafts of afternoon sun filtering across the fallen leaves.

How had she gotten into all this with Gran and Marsh about being engaged? It made her faintly uneasy. There was nothing really specific between her and Barry. Quite the contrary. Barry was explicit in his opinion of marriage and his reluctance to take that step again.

He'd change, wouldn't he? And then he'd be willing

to make a formal as well as an emotional commitment....

But what if he wasn't? Vivi tried to dismiss that small questioning voice. Of course he would be! They weren't like people in their circle, who gave up on a relationship the moment any friction developed. They would work together to overcome the inevitable problems of living together and loving together.

At least *she* was different.

Was she really such an anachronism as Barry teasingly claimed? He kept jokingly threatening to lace her soft drink so her inhibitions would relax and allow her to do what she actually wanted to do. He patronizingly assured her that she was only suffering from timidity or reluctance because she was still a virgin.

How much easier Gran must have had it. When Gran was her age, it was considered natural for girls to wait until marriage, so she hadn't had the peer pressure to struggle against. Did times really change? Were these new ways actually superior?

"Try It, You Might Like It," her co-workers teased. What if she did try it and didn't like it? It might be enjoyable physically, but she'd seen sex without commitment and marriage lead to emotional misery with too many people.

Firmly dismissing all problems which she couldn't solve immediately, Vivi headed for the stairs. She'd better give them a thorough check to be certain that the red spaceship was the only toy Nicky'd dropped. True, she'd been up and down these stairs and along the hall, but she'd been intent upon moving Gran and Marsh. She might have overlooked something.

She had, but not toys on the floor. As she started up the bottom step, she spied her postcards and unsealed letter still lying on the hall table near the phone. She didn't want them cluttering up the neatness of the hall. Vivi scooped up her writing materials and carried them along as she inspected the stairway and corridor.

"Gran—" she said, tapping on the door which had been Marsh's, then opening it a crack. "I'm going for a little walk and to mail these. You'll be all right?"

"Mercy, yes, it was Marsh who fell, not me," Gran reassured. "Writing your young man?" She was stretched out on the bed, the pillows banked behind her curly silver head, the Sunday papers strewn around her, and the magazine section in her hand.

"And my roommate and Mother and Daddy," she nodded. "The post office is still where it used to be, isn't it? By the northwest corner of the square? Anything you want me to do for you while I'm out?"

"Just have yourself a good time," Gran told her. "I'm all set right where I am, and I can hear if Marsh or anyone else needs me. Well—leave my door open, to be sure I do hear."

Vivi took her things on up to the tower room, checked her hair and lipstick, got her purse, and set out. The afternoon was warmer than when they'd walked to the church, but the air was as crisp and fragrant, and the autumn colors were as bright on trees here in town as out in the country.

When she reached the post office, she dropped the cards and letter in the mailbox at the curb, then went on across to the square. On a fine weekend afternoon like this, the courthouse lawn was wall-to-wall people. The entire square was, in fact, and huge tour buses kept rolling in to unload even more.

The Covered Bridge Festival was supposed to be one of the top ten crowd attracters in the entire United

States, up with the Indy 500 and Kentucky Derby, and seeing the square now, Vivi could believe it. She re-crossed a street and made her way back to Gran's quieter neighborhood. Even it was full of parked and hopefully cruising cars.

"I'll see everything through the week, when these crowds thin out a little bit," she said under her breath. "I wish Barry were here. It was more fun yesterday, when I had someone to see it with." Marsh. Yes, he was good company. She liked him.

The O'Haras returned from their sightseeing, reclaimed the mangled red plastic spaceship, and were full of apologies about the accident.

How different from the city, Vivi reflected. Marsh wasn't threatening to sue Gran or the O'Haras. So many people she knew called a lawyer at the drop of a hat. Of course, Marsh might yet. How much could he do on a Sunday afternoon?

But he seemed to understand that small children did drop toys. Gran couldn't keep a constant watch, and he assumed part of the blame himself, saying again he should have watched his step. He had been so frank to say he was watching her.

As evening came, Gran bustled into the kitchen, saying, "We'll have to fix a nice tray for Marsh, won't we? Now where did I put that wicker laptray?"

"Oh—yes," Vivi agreed, taken aback. Rallying, she said, "I think I saw it in the pantry."

Going in to look for it, she wondered if they'd be serving him three meals a day in bed. If she would, that is. Gran would make sure Vivi was the one who took it to him, and maybe even spoon-fed it to him.

Not just the breakfast included with the room. Not even the occasional dinner when she cooked a big batch of something and Gran invited him to stay. But all three meals. Day after day. Every day. He would be watching her play waitress, talking to her, needling her about Barry and her ringless engagement.

Oh, well, it wouldn't last long. The festival itself only lasted another week. He'd leave then. Anyway, he'd be back on his feet well before then, first on the crutches and then navigating without them. Sprained ankles didn't last long.

She set the tray nicely and even added a few late-blooming flowers and colorful autumn leaves to make a little bouquet.

Gran's thick, hearty vegetable soup made ideal invalid fare. Vivi disdained serving crackers with it; she sliced and buttered French bread and sprinkled it with paprika and garlic salt, then toasted it golden brown.

Marsh refused to eat in bed. He hobbled out into the living room on crutches, and Gran quickly served all three of them on the mahogany teacart near his chair.

"What a pity, injuring your ankle right at the beginning of the festival," Gran sympathized. "At least you've had yesterday and today to walk around, and you'd do the sightseeing by car anyway."

"Yes..." Marsh sounded abstracted, dubious. "A business appointment down in Terre Haute's what worries me. I don't know if I can drive with this bad ankle."

"Why not?" Vivi said, briskly encouraging. "It's your left ankle. I can see, with a right ankle, that the brake and accelerator'd be a problem, but—"

"But we drive different cars," he pointed out ruefully. "Yours is automatic, right? Mine's stickshift, manual transmission, which means using the left foot on the clutch whenever I shift."

"Oh. I suppose so." Vivi felt taken aback, embarrassed. She hadn't thought of that.

"That shouldn't be any problem," Gran declared. "You'll be glad to drive him, won't you, Vivi?"

"Me!" Vivi practically yelped it. "Gran, I can't drive a stickshift! I never have, and I'm not about to begin on that expensive sports car!"

"Better not," Marsh concurred, looking alarmed. "I don't want anything happening to you—or to my new car!"

"Well, no, of course not. Mercy sakes!" Gran was indignant. "I didn't mean that! Vivi could take you in her own car. Can't you, Vivi? You'll be glad to."

"I suppose so." Glad? No, definitely not! Her reaction whenever he touched her, when his gaze lingered on her, made her distinctly uneasy.

She couldn't remember exactly how far Terre Haute was, but taking him to keep an appointment and staying with him, then bringing him back here was sure to take a couple of hours, at the very least.

Reluctant to sound rude or ungracious when Marsh really was injured and probably was embarrassed by her grandmother's obvious attempts at matchmaking, Vivi qualified, "If you feel up to it, Marsh. The doctor did say—maybe it would be better for you to reschedule your appointment."

Gran considered that. "See how you feel in the morning," she advised Marsh. "You're the best judge of that."

"I'm sure I'll feel okay," he said positively. "I already feel much better after that nap. I can make it fine if Vivi does the driving. And it is a rather important meeting." His glance at Vivi was appealing.

He seemed faintly concerned about it, and Vivi's

compassionate heart melted. Why not take him? It had been years since she'd even been through Terre Haute. The drive could be interesting, and she had more than enough time to sightsee around Rockville.

"If you feel up to it in the morning, I'll be glad to take you," Vivi firmly assured him. "What time is your meeting? And how far is Terre Haute?"

Ruefully, Marsh shrugged. "Not far—do you have any idea, Mrs. Gordon? At least twenty miles, but not much over thirty, I'd say."

"I have a map out in the car," Vivi offered, getting to her feet. "Hang on. I'll go get it. I need to see what the route is, anyway."

She hurried outdoors, to her little red car, and found the Indiana map in the glove compartment. She'd used an Illinois map to drive here from St. Louis. Instead of taking Interstate 70 from St. Louis, which would have taken her through Terre Haute, she'd taken state highways through Illinois by way of Decatur. There she spent Thursday night with an old school friend who now lived there and worked at WAND-TV, the local television station. From Decatur, it had been Route 36 all the way across to Indiana and Rockville.

Back inside, she drew an ottoman over near Marsh's chair and unfolded the map. With their heads close together studying the map, Vivi was again pleasantly conscious of the warmth of his skin.

"There it is," he said, a lean, tanned forefinger indicating the border city. "Straight down Route 41 from here. I'd say about twenty-five miles, wouldn't you?"

Vivi nodded, unaware that the slight motion wafted her shampoo's fragrance up to his nostrils, too. "A little over half an hour to drive, most likely. What time is your appointment?"

"Ten-thirty. So, if we start at nine-thirty, a quarter-to-ten, that would give us plenty of time to get to Terre Haute." He raised a questioning dark brow at her.

Vivi nodded again. It would, and she would also be able to help Gran with the morning breakfast and housekeeping chores before they started.

"Then we can have lunch down there before we come back," he planned aloud. "I'll buy your gas and lunch, of course."

"Oh, no," Vivi demurred. "That isn't necessary. I'm glad to do it." And to her surprise, she discovered she was. Only a few minutes ago, she'd felt reluctant, but somehow now she anticipated the trip. When—and why had her feelings changed?

"Well, you're not going to," he declared. "You're doing it to help me, not because you already meant to go there. The least I can do is pay the expenses. I ought to pay you for your time and trouble, too."

"Oh no!" she protested, alarmed. "All right, you can pay for lunch and fuel, if it makes you feel better, but you really needn't." She smiled at him, surrendering gracefully.

The evening ended early. For all of Marsh's claims that he felt much better, he looked weary and soon retired to his room. None of the other guests stayed out late or wanted to watch television long after coming in. Bed-and-breakfast establishments catered to family trade; sophisticates stayed at motels or down in Terre Haute, where there'd be some night life.

Vivi was more than willing to climb up to her little nest high in the tower. The stairs seemed long and steep tonight.

What a day this had been! She thought back over the morning bustle to get everything done before going to

59

church. The afternoon had been peaceful enough—until Marsh's fall. Poor guy! Again her mind gave a flashback of his fall, how he'd looked sprawled unconscious, and how worn he seemed this evening.

She should be more generous about his motives. It wasn't his fault Gran was an inveterate matchmaker! And if he was attracted to her and showed it even though he knew she was interested only in someone else, that was flattering. A trifle annoying at times, but still flattering.

Briskly she turned down her bed and changed to her nightgown, anticipating snuggling down and reading for a while before turning out the light. There was no more pleasant way to make the transition from the day's activities to sleep than losing herself in a lively story as she relaxed and grew sleepy.

Had she left her books this way? The paperbacks were at the back of the shelf, and the new Bible was at the front. Vivi felt certain she'd left them just the opposite. Had Gran been up here and rearranged them as a not-too-subtle hint?

Frowning, Vivi changed them back to the way she preferred. She wished Gran wouldn't do that.

Going to church had been a pleasant enough experience, but being pressured in any way antagonized her. She was a grown woman, successful in a career, able to decide for herself, and she resented being manipulated, even by a loving grandmother who just wanted to pair her off with a nice man or share a new Bible.

Then she shrugged, hand still on the Bible, and she gave it an almost caressing little rub. Dipping into it would make Gran happy and certainly wouldn't hurt her. Gran wouldn't live forever, so any little thing Vivi could do to make her happy....

Besides, Vivi'd read reviews and debates about whether a modern version of the Bible helped or harmed it. She was rather curious to see for herself what it was like. If she could satisfy her curiosity and make Gran happy at the same time, why not?

"But not tonight," she said under her breath, easing between the sheets and picking up the half-finished romance which lay open and face down. "I've got to see how Brandi and Giorgio come out in Venice first!"

Chapter Five

"Can you make it?" Vivi asked with concern. Her hand went out apprehensively. She wanted to help Marsh but feared any touch might unbalance him.

"If you take your crutches—?" Gran suggested.

Marsh grinned, teetering on one foot by the open door of Vivi's little red car. "Good thing we allowed extra time. We may need it, just getting me in and out of this thing! Yes—here, Mrs. G. I think I can manage better without them now."

Inserting his long body into the small confines of the car was no easy job, particularly with the necessity of protecting his lame left ankle. Finally he was in, and his crutches angled into the back seat behind him.

"Made it!" Vivi said with satisfaction. "Okay, Gran, expect us when you see us."

"Mid-afternoon, most likely," Marsh added. "Okay, ma'am, ready when you are!"

Laughing a trifle breathlessly, Vivi hurried around to get in at the wheel, smooth her skirt, and turn the key in the ignition. Getting started had become quite a project, with various other cars having to be moved so Vivi's could leave the drive.

Rockville traffic was far lighter this Monday than it had been all weekend, and Vivi headed away from the busy square, not toward it. Soon she was on Route 36, and almost immediately at the intersection with Route 41 and signaling to make a left onto it.

"Well, I'm getting to see some of the fall foliage," Marsh commented philosophically, as they took the hilly, winding road southward. "I don't suppose anything on the tour routes would be more scenic than this."

"It's lovely," Vivi concurred, "but are there any covered bridges along it? I've never been to New England, but this is how I've always imagined it must be."

"It can't be better than this," Marsh declared. "There's a little white church up here that looks straight out of New England, too. There it is."

"Oh, nice," Vivi approved. "Harmony Church—what a good name for it. It looks so serene and right in this setting, doesn't it?"

They drove in companionable silence for a while, except for calling one another's attention to a particularly beautiful gold, crimson, or orange tree. The highway looped through the landscape, enforcing a moderate pace even on a clear morning. From time to time they came to small towns, slowing to go through them and then picking up speed once more. The fine morning, colorful scenery, and friendly quiet inside the car were all unexpectedly pleasant.

"Not much farther now," Marsh eventually remarked, as they left the highway behind and entered a stretch of freeway for the last miles into the city.

"You'll have to direct me to where we're going," Vivi told him. "I don't know Terre Haute at all. I've been through there, but with my parents, and I didn't pay attention to the streets or landmarks."

"Yes, I know how it is; passengers don't," he assented. "It's an easy place to find."

"What is it?" Vivi asked curiously. "We talked a lot about my job—was that only yesterday afternoon? So much has happened since then, it seems like days ago! But you didn't tell me what you do or where we're going."

"Didn't I? I suppose because your grandmother knows all about it, I thought you did, too. We're in related fields, actually. Advertising. You write it at a TV station; I'm a partner in an ad agency. And sales manager. The other partners are family men, they don't care for travel and sales, so it evolved that I'd take that aspect of the business.

"We're going to a television station now, as a matter of fact. You'll be interested in seeing how it compares to the one where you work. Then if we can fit it in, I'd like to make a quick call at a radio station, too."

"Sure. I don't know why not," Vivi said cooperatively. "Advertising, really? That's a coincidence. I'm surprised Gran didn't mention it."

It almost seemed too much of a coincidence. She wondered again about her grandmother's tactics. But, she thought with amusement, selling advertising certainly went with scarlet Corvettes. His agency must be prospering, though that didn't always follow. Salesmen often spent a disproportionately large slice of income on clothes and cars to present precisely such a successful image.

"Yes, since she told me that you write advertising, I thought perhaps she'd told you I do, too. Small world? My agency specializes in Christian advertising."

Sounding amused, he added, "Now if you tell me you do, too—!"

Vivi laughed. "No—no, I don't." Inwardly, she debated: act knowledgeable and wonder, or admit her ignorance and find out? Curiosity won. "Christian advertising? I don't think I've heard of that. Unless, of course, by a different name."

"It's a comparatively new field, so you probably haven't," he said comfortably. "Christian publications and radio and TV stations have been springing up in recent years. Ordinary ad agencies aren't successful in writing for them; the slant is all wrong, both in copy and visuals. So Christian ad agencies were developed to meet that need.

"It isn't the easiest thing in the world to create. It takes more than a good ad man or a good Christian to hit the right blend." His tone turned teasing. "Now, if you were more religious than you say—and not engaged to good old Barry—I'd try to recruit you."

Vivi laughed, "Afraid not. I'm happy where I am, and if I'm good at writing copy there, probably I wouldn't meet your standards. I would like to know more about what constitutes good Christian advertising, though." It sounded dull to her, yet Marsh didn't seem dull, and anyhow, her curiosity still demanded satisfaction.

"Later," he promised. "Who knows, you and Barry may split up, and you may want to give it a try? But for now, here's Terre Haute, so we'd better concentrate on finding the TV station."

Locating it wasn't difficult. Marsh was an excellent guide, telling her in advance where to change lanes in preparation to make a turn. For that matter, he was a better passenger than most men. Barry was a—well, dashing—driver, and on the rare occasions he'd ridden with her, he'd teased her about her caution.

Getting Marsh out of the little car was even harder than getting him in, since gravity was now against them. When he finally did get up and onto one good foot, he overbalanced and wavered, about to fall.

Vivi made a grab, threw her arms about him, and braced herself. He grabbed back, hugging her, and for a moment they staggered together, laughing a little, before they ended up balanced against the side of the car.

"Hey, you do a mean polka," he teased, hazel eyes glinting down at her, kissing-close.

"Polka! I was trying to do a Texas two-step," she gasped at random. "Are you really crippled or just making a pass? Let go, and I'll get your crutches." She was breathless, laughing—and immensely glad that she had managed to keep him from falling.

"Ahh, you're on to me," he grieved. "I thought it was a pretty neat cover for getting my arms around you, myself."

"Take your crutches," she ordered severely. "You'll be late for your appointment." She watched while he adjusted them to fit comfortably under his arms. "Shall I wait out here in the car for you?"

"Why don't you come in with me?" he suggested. "Wouldn't you like to see the station, compare it with where you work? I'm sure they'd be glad to give you the grand tour."

"Well, yes, actually, I would," Vivi admitted. "Er—you mentioned Christian publications and stations. Is this one of them?"

"Nope, this's just a regular station." He grinned at her. "There isn't that much difference, Vivi. You'd be comfortable in either one."

66

This station was smaller than the one where Vivi worked, but she immediately felt at home. There was the same friendly, joking atmosphere, the crew teasing Marsh about his crutches and chauffeur. He repeated his claim that he'd been felled by a hostile alien space-ship, which caused more hilarity.

A perky blonde from the continuity department was assigned to show Vivi around while Marsh and various executives conferred. She saw the studio, the art and copy offices, and the staff lounge where they helped themselves to coffee.

Busily she and her guide compared notes and topped one another's anecdotes about wild characters and zany happenings. They even discovered they knew a few of the same people. Announcers tended to change jobs fairly often, one man in particular circu-lated constantly, either changing or revisiting places he had worked in hopes of finding something better. He wasn't popular, especially among the women, and one at Vivi's station locked herself into her office for the duration of each visit he made.

A phone call summoned the blonde guide away, and Vivi remained in the lounge, thoughtfully sipping her coffee and wondering whether there were characters of that sort in Christian broadcasting, as well. Were they true, committed Christians, or had they simply discovered a good thing, a wide-open new field?

The same question applied to Marsh. Had he been sincere in talking about faith yesterday afternoon out on the porch swing and this morning in the car? Per-haps she'd misjudged him in thinking he was pretend-ing because he knew Gran to be deeply religious and assumed Vivi would be, too. This would be another reason Gran liked him so well. And Vivi knew that her grandmother was ordinarily an excellent judge of character.

However, Gran hadn't been forced to develop a big city shell of cynicism. She wouldn't distrust a presentable young man, a fellow Christian, who had stayed with her during several previous festivals. Why should she?

However, Vivi had worked and lived in a large city long enough to wonder about Marshall Henderson automatically. His clothes and car showed he made good money. His devotion could be lip service to the excellent living made by getting in on the ground floor of a new field. Most men were loyal to their careers.

What did it matter, anyway? They were only casual acquaintances, friends, because he was one of Gran's guests and in need of special assistance due to his injured ankle.

Well, there was a trifle more to it than that, honesty made her concede. He was an extremely attractive man. She enjoyed the time she spent with him. If she didn't have Barry, she could get quite bright-eyed over him.

"Sorry to keep you waiting," the blonde apologized, returning. "I had to hunt up some copy in the files and read it back to him. So you and Marsh don't work together now. How about in the future? Any chance?"

Vivi shrugged, smiling. "I doubt it. All my family and friends are in the St. Louis area, plus a pretty special guy. I don't foresee leaving them. Marsh is based in Paducah, you know."

"I know. I wouldn't mind if he moved up here," the girl observed, blue eyes sparkling. "Now, he's one all the gals at the station look forward to seeing. No one locks herself away when he comes around. And he's nice, too. I just hate the salesmen who are all hands and full of suggestive remarks, don't you?"

Vivi's glance was expressive. Before she could reply, however, the phone rang with a message that Marsh had completed his business.

Getting him back into the car was another occasion for hilarity, as various people aided and advised. Vivi stood back and left it to them, but at last both Marsh and his crutches were settled, and she got in and started the engine.

"Now—lunch?" he suggested. "What sounds good to you and where?"

Vivi glanced at him, making a face of humorous dismay. "Hey, I'm the stranger in town, remember? You've been here before; you tell me."

"Honey Creek Mall has a good cafeteria, but I don't think I'm up to that with crutches," he said thoughtfully. "Can you see me carrying a tray?"

"I'd rather not see you carrying a tray," Vivi declared, shuddering. "Perhaps we should avoid crowded places, as well. Mmm...let's see...what does that leave? A drive-in?"

"You just don't want to get me in and out of this car again," Marsh teased.

"So next time get rescued by somebody who drives a van," Vivi retorted. "I'm game. I think I'm even beginning to get the hang of it."

Eventually they settled on a cheerful, small Mexican restaurant where they could park right at the door and Marsh could get inside and sit down with a minimum of trouble.

"I like it here, and the food's good," Marsh said, looking a trifle apologetic at taking her to a fast-food restaurant rather than an expensive place with plush decor.

"It's a treat to me," Vivi assured him, inhaling with pleasure. "I like Mexican food, and I don't get it often."

"Don't tell me, I can guess—Barry doesn't like it," Marsh surmised, with a knowing glance.

"Well, not everyone does, you know," Vivi defended. "And there aren't any Mexican places close to either the TV station or where I live."

They ordered at the counter, with Marsh insisting upon a lavish assortment of foods. Then Vivi helped to settle him at a convenient table before going back to get their trays when their number was called.

"I know a couple of good Mexican places in St. Louis," he said thoughtfully, as she spread out the meal on the table between them. "We'll go eat there when I'm in town. Where else do you like to eat? If you like Mexican, do you like Szechuan Chinese, too? It's hot with pepper."

"I've never tried it, just Mandarin and Cantonese," Vivi responded, carefully avoiding either agreeing or disagreeing to dinner together in St. Louis. She was sure he'd never get around to it.

In fact, she realized, she was taking all of his attention too seriously. Heavens, he was a salesman! As soon as Marsh Henderson returned to active health and his normal life, he'd forget all about her.

Barry was a salesman, too. Did he—? Maybe. Just in the line of business. Vivi was confident that he meant it when he told her how much he loved her. He proved it by how much time he spent with her.

Abruptly, Vivi felt dismayed and discouraged. She tried to tell herself it was only because her taco shell crumbled, its filling spilling onto her plate and lap, making her look like a klutz. Or because of the thought that Barry might lightly flirt with other girls. Not because Marsh flirted, too, and soon would forget her.

Marsh was laughing at the mess on her lap, but it was friendly laughter, and as if in retribution, his taco disintegrated, too.

"Where would we be without paper napkins?" he chuckled. He wadded up the napkin which had been in his lap and caught the fallen food. "This's the one thing I don't like about Mexican food. I drop as much as I eat."

"Oh, not quite as much," Vivi teased back, overcoming her momentary depression. "But I'll be a sport. I'll let you have the last taco."

"You only say that because you like enchiladas better," he accused, spreading a fresh napkin to protect his slacks.

"Behave yourself," she admonished, "Or I won't help you in and out of the car, and then where'll you be?"

"You sure know how to hurt a guy," he complained pitifully. The dancing gleam in his eyes ruined the effect of his mournful expression and doleful tone. He gave up and grinned at her. "Yes, ma'am. Anything you say, ma'am. I'll be a perfect gentleman."

"Well, nobody's perfect," she granted. "I'm not asking the impossible of you." They laughed together, relaxed and comfortable. Then she said, "I'm really intrigued by what you were telling me earlier, before we got clear into Terre Haute, about the kind of advertising you do. I've never heard or seen any of it—unless, of course, I have without realizing it. Tell me more. Or, do you have any samples along that I could see?"

"I do, but they're in my attaché case, out in the car," he told her. "Sure. I'll be glad to show them to you. Who knows, we may recruit you yet?"

"Oh, I doubt that," Vivi protested. "I told you, I'm happy where I am. I'm curious, that's all."

"Later," he promised. "At the station, or back at your grandmother's house. I almost said back home. It feels like home there, doesn't it?" He glanced at the thin gold watch on his strong wrist. "And now, do you suppose we should think about starting on?"

"Possibly," Vivi agreed. "Yes, considering that it takes us a minute or two to get you into the car, and out again when we get there. How about this radio station? Ordinary or Christian?"

"This one's Christian. You'll enjoy seeing it, too," he assured her. "Nice place, nice people who buy the very best in advertising." His grin was self-mocking.

"Yes, and you pride yourself on your humility," Vivi said dryly, her glance teasing. She rose and reached to steady him as he levered himself up from their table.

He really was becoming adept with his crutches by now, swinging along easily once he was up on his feet. And, Vivi thought with affectionate admiration, he somehow gave the impression that he'd been injured doing some adventurous act of heroism. Marsh Henderson had style, no doubt about it.

"I don't believe I've ever been to any radio station at all, before now," Vivi remarked thoughtfully, when they were in the car, driving toward it. "Are they very different from TV stations?"

"Well, their broadcasting studios don't have cameras and lights and sets. Other than that, they're pretty much alike. You'll see."

Vivi did see. Again she got a special tour of the small station, and although there were differences, enough similarities existed to make her feel at home.

Marsh received the same warm welcome as he had at the television station, and so did she, because she was with him. The friendly young woman who showed her around this station was also curious, if tactful, about her relationship with Marsh, about whether she worked with him or was his girl.

"Just his chauffeur," Vivi said, lightly yet firmly. "He can't drive that sports car of his with a bad ankle." She grinned impishly. "In fact, I don't know how he could even get in and out of it, low-slung as it is."

A monitor speaker was on in the waiting room, and Vivi recognized a program as one which Gran often listened to on the little kitchen radio. Vivi hadn't paid any particular attention then, and she couldn't concentrate on it now, not when people were talking to her. She wondered fleetingly, before being completely distracted by the conversation, whether any of the commercials she'd heard had been written by Marsh.

As back at the station where she worked, there were posters on the walls, plaques with humorous slogans, and some awards. Only gradually did she notice that most of these were of a religious nature—*With Christ, all things are possible* and *Please be patient; God isn't finished with me yet*. She liked a big poster on one office wall, *Grant me patience, Lord—and I want it RIGHT NOW!*

By the time they got into the car for the last time, Vivi's concerned eye noticed that Marsh looked tired

and a little drawn, even though it was barely midafter-
noon.

"Head acting up? Or your leg bothering you?" she
questioned anxiously.

"My head does ache some," he admitted cautiously.
"But nothing I can't live with. I should've thought to
take an aspirin back there."

"I have some in my purse, if you can swallow pills
without water," she offered. "Water—I don't know
where we'd find that."

"I can. It might do double duty and help my ankle,
too," he said gratefully. "It doesn't feel as good as it
might."

"Help yourself, then." With one hand on the steer-
ing wheel, she passed him her large bag from the floor
of the car. "Mmmm—you may have to hunt for them,
but they're in there someplace, in a little flat box."

Although Vivi kept her attention on driving, she was
fully aware of his rummaging through her small neces-
sities until he pulled out the pillbox. There was something oddly companionable and intimate about his
search through her belongings, just as there had been
to sharing food this noon and her packing and unpacking for him yesterday.

This won't do, she warned herself. It wouldn't do at
all to start feeling close to this man, particularly when
she knew he was a salesman, when she was unlikely
ever to see him again after this week, and when Barry
was already hypersensitive about what he saw as a
woman's betrayal.

Oh, nonsense! She was making far too much of this.
She and Marsh were only casual friends. She'd feel the
same if he were a child or a senior citizen whom she
was helping. Well, sort of the same. The fact that he

was an extremely attractive man was bound to make some difference.

"I'm glad to be back out in the countryside," she remarked a little later, as they left Terre Haute behind and got away from the stretch of divided highway.

"You like the country and small towns better?" Marsh asked with casual interest.

"It's a nice change. After all, life in a large city is pretty hectic." She gave him a brief, keenly assessing glance. "You look and sound better. The aspirin must have taken effect."

"Yes. It was a big help. Thanks." He turned to be able to look at her rather than the road. "You're a real friend, Vivi. I couldn't have kept those appointments today without your help. True, the radio station was only tentative, but it turned out to be as good as the TV station." A strong brow quirked ruefully, as he admitted, "Even if I'd had automatic transmission in the 'vette, I didn't have any business behind the wheel today. I intend to do something to repay you."

"I didn't do it for that," Vivi protested. "I was glad to be able to help you, and it's been very interesting. I really enjoyed seeing those stations and finding out how they're different and similar to the one where I work."

"All the same, you gave up a whole day of your vacation," he insisted. "You must have had other plans, which you sacrificed."

Vivi shrugged. It always made her uncomfortable to receive praise beyond what she actually deserved. "Nothing much. Taking another look around the square, perhaps, and driving around one of the bridge routes. There are only four of those, and none of them takes terribly long to tour. I still have the rest of this week to do that. The weekend—" She made a little grimace.

"Yeah, bumper-to-bumper traffic again," he drawled. "The scenery's bound to be beautiful this year. We can tell that, just from here on the highway."

"Yes, but the covered bridges are on the back roads, for the most part," Vivi pointed out.

Abruptly she realized that she could meander around those back roads, seeing the autumn color and all those quaint bridges, with stops at the little towns which had their own festival events in full swing all week long, but what was Marsh going to do?

She could envision him all too clearly, lounging about in the living room or stretched out on his bed. Reading. Watching television. Possibly studying the work in his briefcase. Talking to Gran. But while he did have business in the area, his primary reason for staying in Rockville was to see that scenery, too.

An active man like Marsh would be bored stiff by the enforced idleness, yet trapped there until his ankle was well enough for him to drive his sports car. And how many days would that be?

"Look," she offered, before she could think better of it, "why don't you come along with me?"

"Haven't you put up with enough today, getting me in and out of your car?" he queried wryly.

She gestured magnanimously. "I'm getting the hang of it! You want to see the country roads and bridges, don't you?"

"I thought maybe I could get to the square, somehow, and go on one of the bus tours."

"You've got to be kidding!" she gasped. "It may not be much of a walk to the square ordinarily, but on crutches? And have you really thought that out? Getting up the steps of a bus, and along one of those narrow aisles when you've got a bad ankle and crutches to maneuver?"

"You're probably right," he conceded. "Still, I don't want to be a drag on you."

"You wouldn't be." Vivi spoke firmly, wondering at the same time about the advisability of spending so much time with him. Still, Gran would like the idea and as long as she and Marsh both knew that this was platonic friendship, nothing more, let Gran be pleased. "It's always more fun doing something with someone than alone—and how could I enjoy myself, knowing you were stuck back at the house, grounded?"

"Oh well, I wouldn't want to give you a guilty conscience," Marsh said, laughter in his voice. "If you're sure, then I accept, with gratitude."

"Unless I'm putting you on the spot, pressuring you into it?" Vivi said, struck by sudden doubt.

"Hey!" he protested, indignant. "You should know you're not. You're dead right. Anything is more enjoyable if you share it with a friend. Today's been fun, hasn't it?"

"Yes, it has." *Unexpectedly so*, she thought.

"So," he said with satisfaction. "There's just one thing left to decide: what time do you want to start? Two things, come to think of it—what time, and which of the routes? Got a favorite?"

Vivi shrugged, wondering at her heightened sense of anticipation. "About the same time as we did today? And we can study the festival map and decide on the route between now and then."

"Good," he said. "Yeah. We'll get our heads together. You know, this may turn out to be the best festival yet.''

Vivi smiled and nodded silently. She found she was looking forward to tomorrow very much. Mere sightseeing had suddenly turned into an adventure.

Chapter Six

"Welcome back! Did you have a good day?" Gran called. Plainly she had been sitting in her favorite porch rocker and watching for them. She rose and hurried down the steps and across the lawn as soon as Vivi eased to a stop in the drive.

"Very successful," Marsh assured her. "Look how well I can get out of this car now."

"Where is everyone?" Vivi asked, surveying the almost-empty drive. Only Marsh's Corvette and a Ford station wagon were parked there now, in contrast to its usual crowded condition.

"Out sightseeing, most likely. The Culbersons," Gran nodded at the wagon, "are out on foot. And the new folks aren't in yet. My, yes, Marsh, you're getting real spry. I hope you don't have trouble with those front steps."

"I'll manage," he promised her. "You going to catch me if I fall?"

"That'd be a sight to see," she said tartly, eyes twinkling. "A big man like you are, you'd mash me flat if you fell on me. Marsh, your office called a little bit ago, and they'd like you to call back. And, Vivi, you've got a letter from your young man."

"Oh really?" Vivi asked, intrigued. She hadn't expected Barry to write her, certainly not so soon. But how very gratifying! Sometimes she got the feeling that neither Gran nor Marsh actually believed in his existence.

Both Vivi and Gran held their breath while Marsh slowly negotiated the steps up to the porch. They exhaled, sharing a glance of relief as he limped on over to the front door. Vivi followed, carrying his attaché case.

Barry's letter lay on the hall table near the telephone. As soon as Marsh was settled in the chair by the phone, she carried the envelope into the living room. It was from Barry, all right. She recognized his careless scrawl, even before seeing his name and address on the upper left corner.

Curling up on the comfortable old sofa, she tore off the envelope's end, careful not to tear into the letter itself. Aside from scrawled notes left on her desk at work, this was the first letter she'd had from Barry. She would read it to Gran, to show Gran that Barry really did love her, even if she wasn't wearing his ring.

And if Marsh Henderson overheard, maybe it would prove something to him, as well.

Oh. Except for the careless scrawl of his name, he'd written it on his new plaything, a funny little ultra-light typewriter with hard-to-read dot-matrix print. Somehow it robbed the letter of some of the romance. Oh, well, it was the thought that counted, and what he said in it.

Hi, Sweets
How are things out in the boondogs? Bet your realy bored by now. Miss me? I sure do miss you.

You missed a great party last nite. A real swinger. It didn't brake up till almost dawn, and I've got the grandaddy of all hangovers. Tony did his Boy George imitation. Its my turn to throw the next one. How about making it a housewarming for *our* new pad? Listen, I hope your doing some heavy thinking about that. You know it doesn't make any sense, each of us having the expense of an apartment & you worrying about finding a new roommate, not when we're crazy about each other. It isnt healthy or natural. You've got to grow up & get over some of those hang-ups of yours & start living in the real world. Well I better get going. I miss you & hope you miss me somewhere near as much. Maybe we'll see each other sooner than we thot, huh?

Bye

Barry.

Vivi sat staring at the page for a moment after she finished reading it. She certainly couldn't show that letter to either Gran or Marsh. She'd even have difficulty reading a censored version aloud.

In dot-matrix print, it all looked so much different from actually seeing Barry say it, his expression so earnest, a teasing twinkle in his blue eyes. Typed, it looked flat and cold, as if he were talking down to her. It was funny that as a copywriter she'd never noticed how often he repeated some words, and either misspelled—or maybe merely mistyped—others.

Vivi suddenly realized she hadn't heard any of the casual, suggestive banter so common around the television station since she'd been here at Gran's. Marsh didn't sprinkle his conversation with it.

81

She was also glad she'd missed that party. In fact, she'd left a day early just to avoid it. She wished she could miss the one Barry anticipated giving. She couldn't, of course. She'd have to help prepare for it and serve as hostess, but it was *not* going to be a housewarming to celebrate living together.

Those parties invariably lasted too long and some of the people drank too much, and their antics were hilarious only to the others who drank heavily, embarrassing to the ones who didn't.

Vivi frowned at the letter. She wasn't judging them. It was their life, and if that was how they wanted to live, she wasn't stopping them. Barry was the judgmental one, always picking at her. For somebody who claimed to love everything about her, he certainly criticized her a lot.

"Not bad news, I hope?" Gran asked, concerned.

"Hmmm? Oh, no, no. He just misses me and wishes I'd been there to go to a party with him." Folding the page and sliding it back into its envelope, then into her purse, Vivi saw Marsh move away from the phone to join them. He must have overheard her brief description. She smiled at him. "Not trouble back at the office, I hope?"

"No, good news, if anything," he told them. However, he didn't look overjoyed. "We landed an account we've been wanting."

"Oh, that is good," Vivi said, pleased for him. Nothing made a salesman or agency happier, so why didn't he look more cheerful? It had to be that his ankle bothered him or his head ached again; by now the aspirin must have worn off.

Or he might just be wishing he were back at his office, at work, instead of stuck here with a bad ankle, unable to drive or do anything productive, dependent upon her assistance.

"Yes, Steve knew I'd like to know the details and start mulling over the ad campaign before I got back to the office." He began to look more relaxed and pleased, a light in his eyes as he considered it.

"Do you already have ideas for it?" she asked, interested. "Don't forget you were going to show me some of your copy. I really would like to see your work."

He smiled. "There's one in that magazine of your grandmother's," he told her, nodding toward the latest issue of *Christian Herald*, lying on the coffee table. "I have some vague ideas the direction I want to go with this new one. Nothing specific yet. I—"

"Lookit what I got!" Young Nicky O'Hara burst in, waving an old-fashioned wooden toy. Vivi remembered having seen the booth which sold them in the courthouse craft tent. "D'you know how to work it, Marsh? Do you? I do!"

"From spaceships to this," Mrs. O'Hara murmured to Vivi, face expressive, watching Nicky demonstrate his toy.

Other guests began coming in, some returning from a full day, tired but happy, and new ones arriving to check in, full of anticipation.

"Later," Marsh told Vivi, with a significant glance at the magazine and his attaché case. "We've got all week, haven't we?"

Showing the guests to bedrooms and baths and explaining whatever they needed to know had become Vivi's job. She was kept busy hurrying up the stairs with one group, then back down to greet the next set.

Gran was then free to answer the door and act as hostess, telling the guests which events were available during the evening. Tonight, for instance, the Parke County Choral Club and the Bill Swern Slide Show were at the Ritz Theatre. Other nights the Parke Players presented an old-fashioned melodrama.

"What say we try that sometime?" Marsh suggested to Vivi as she caught her breath between climbs up the stairs. "I hear that with the 'mellerdrammer,' the audience boos and hisses the villain and yells warnings to the innocent young heroine. Okay?"

"Fine," Vivi consented, her eyes sparkling. She fanned herself with one slim hand. "Sounds like fun to me—if I survive. I don't know how Gran does it. She can trot up and down those steps without even breathing hard!" She cast a teasing glance her grandmother's way.

"You're from the elevator generation. I'm not," Gran immediately retorted. "I've been climbing up and down those steps too many years to be fazed by them now. Have you read any of that Bible yet?"

"Not yet, but I will, I promise," Vivi assured her. She looked at the attaché case and stack of magazines. "You're not just trying to get out of showing me your work?" she lightly accused Marsh. "I really am interested in it."

"Hey, we're getting a full schedule," he quipped back. He listed on his fingers, "Driving the bridge routes, showing you how to do Christian advertising, and going to the theater. I don't lead that full a social life back home!"

"Neither do I, actually," Vivi said ruefully. "The excitements of life in the big city are sadly overrated. I expect a girl who lives and works right here in Rockville may have as much fun."

"People in big cities tend to be faceless strangers,"

Marsh commented. "In small towns, they know each other. You'd like Paducah. You ought to come see it sometime. It isn't that far from St. Louis or here. It's a nice old river town. Paddlewheel steamboats like the *Delta Queen* stop at the dock. Of course, the *Delta Queen* goes to St. Louis, too. Ever see it there?"

"No. Actually, I don't get over to the Mississippi often," Vivi answered. "My parents live on the west side of town out in the suburbs, so aside from coming to see Gran, I usually go that direction. Paducah—that's a nice name. Indian?"

"I'm not sure. I think so. There are Indian things all around. I'll find out when I get home and tell you when you come visit."

"If I only get to the St. Louis riverfront once in a blue moon, what makes you think I'll ever get to Paducah?" she asked wryly. "Dreamer!"

She got up and hurried to the front door to greet more people. By her reckoning, these were the last to arrive. She hoped so. Today had been a strain. And she was hungrier than she'd supposed possible after such a large lunch.

After she showed the middle-aged couple their room upstairs, Vivi went up to her tower room and changed to sandals, jeans, and her favorite red T-shirt. She freshened up in her pleasantly outdated bathroom, combed her hair, and put on lipstick which exactly matched her shirt. Then, paperback novel in hand, she came down the narrow back stairs.

Gran was in the kitchen, starting supper preparations while the radio on the counter murmured news and weather. Vivi had expected Marsh to be back here with Gran, since she hadn't seen him in the living room, but he was nowhere to be seen.

"He's having a little rest in his room," Gran explained. "I think he feels worse than he wants to admit."

"He mentioned a headache, as we left Terre Haute, and he was very willing to take an aspirin," Vivi told her. "I imagine you're right, and he did—and does—feel worse than he'll own up to. I don't think he's the hypochondriac type, to make a fuss over nothing." She'd suspected that yesterday, but she'd changed her mind.

"We'll call him when it's time to eat. And you're going sightseeing tomorrow, did he say?"

"Yes, but I'll make sure it doesn't turn into such a tiring day," Vivi said, firmly purposeful. "Why should he sit around here, when I'm going to drive a route or two? He can go along, easy as not—and you quit grinning, you sly old fox!"

"Now is that any way for you to talk to your poor old grandma?" she asked reproachfully, but her eyes twinkled, and she couldn't keep her expression severe.

"Oh, Gran!" Vivi exclaimed, as they laughed together, "I had a tour of this radio station of yours. It was one of the places Marsh needed to go. Did you know that? They gave me the grand tour—the nicest people."

"That's just how I thought they'd be," Gran said, pleased. "Did you meet this announcer? Or maybe he's on another shift. And there's a man in the mornings, with the nicest voice—now let me think, what was his name—?"

They made casual conversation as they prepared the food and set the table. Vivi tried to describe the station and its personnel to Gran, but she didn't always remember names, and Gran, of course, only knew names, not how they looked.

Vivi kept alert for the house guests, in case anyone needed something. Footsteps descended the stairs, and there were voices, and the front door opened and closed as people went out to dinner at the local restaurants, but nobody asked for more information. Soon Vivi and Gran had the house to themselves once more.

"Now then!" Gran said with satisfaction, surveying the bowls of salad and the vegetable medley and steaming ham-and-potato casserole she'd just lifted out of the oven. "I do believe that's it. Run call Marsh, will you?"

Marsh didn't need any calling. Vivi found him up on his crutches, crossing the living room, following the aroma of good home cooking toward the comfortable big kitchen.

The three of them felt like a family, Vivi realized as the meal progressed, and she also realized how much she'd missed the easy give-and-take of family life. She enjoyed her independence and liked her roommate, but she and Jill tended only to grab a quick snack in passing or to stick something frozen in the microwave, then eat on trays while watching television. When one was in, the other was generally going out or eating at a different time, hurrying to get ready for a date or meeting. Casual and fast-paced, but what a pleasant change this evening was, sitting at the table with Marsh and Gran, discussing their day. Marsh could supply the names Vivi hadn't caught and tell both of them more about the people at the station.

Marsh lingered, watching and talking, while Vivi and Gran washed and dried the dishes the old-fashioned way, by hand, and tidied up the kitchen.

When the kitchen was back to rights, they moved to the living room, where they watched television for a while. When the program changed, however, none of the new ones appealed to them, so they sat talking, not ready yet to call it a day.

"You were going to show me some of your work," Vivi reminded Marsh.

He winked at Gran. "Hey, I'm beginning to think I have a convert here. Okay. There'll never be a better time."

"Well, if I don't find out, I'll always wonder," Vivi defended herself, and when he began to rise from the sofa, reaching for his crutches, she protested. "No, stay where you are! What do you want? Your attaché case? I'll get it, if you'll just tell me where it is."

"In the bedroom, either on the chair or between the chair and the bed," he responded, leaning back. "That's an offer I won't refuse. Thanks, Vivi."

She found the case with ease. Somehow the bedroom seemed far more masculine now, though it was virtually unchanged.

Marsh patted the cushion next to him on the sofa, and Vivi went to sit there with him. He opened the attaché case, putting it on the coffee table in front of them, and also reached for the *Christian Herald* magazine he'd indicated earlier.

"Now to show you some of my masterpieces," he said, with a self-mocking gleam in his hazel eyes.

"Would you listen to the man!" Vivi appealed to Gran. "You pride yourself on your humility, right?"

"Hey, I believe in telling the truth, the whole truth, and nothing but the truth. Now, be honest: do you watch for the spots you've written?"

"I have to monitor to be sure they're run with the

proper visuals," she claimed, in mock virtue.

"Sure you do. Su-u-ure you do," he drawled, with a knowing twinkle.

"Seems to me you two are well met," Gran commented, enjoying the raillery.

Even though the broadcasting stations had been attractive and professional, and the cover of this magazine was as slickly contemporary as any on the newsstands, Vivi vaguely expected some amateurish, church-bulletin type of format. But the magazine ad for a treasury of gospel music which Marsh showed her was so beautifully photographed and convincingly written that Vivi pored over it in admiration.

Copy from the attaché case covered two lines of books—an appealing group of juveniles and some biblical novels which sounded so interesting Vivi forgot they were designated as inspirational fiction.

"You've sold me," she said wryly, glancing up with a smile. "but somehow, I don't think they're precisely the sort I usually read or listen to."

"I'm not much on reading romances or children's books myself, but the women in our office and Steven's wife gave them rave reviews. I'd be interested in knowing how they strike you, since as you say, they aren't your usual fare."

That's a nice way to call me a heathen, Vivi supposed. No. Marsh wouldn't shoot zingers at her. She was still uncertain whether he was in Christian advertising because of deep conviction on his part or because he made good money from it, but she was becoming increasingly sure that he was a genuinely fine, considerate man.

"Hey, I like this one!" she declared, laughing, as she studied still another layout. The humor in it was good-natured and infectious, making its sales points with swift effectiveness.

"I'm kind of fond of that one, myself," Marsh admitted, pleased, and modest for all his earlier mock boasting. "*And* of this one—"

As they examined and discussed various ads, she was intensely aware of the strength in his lean, tanned arms as he turned a page or pointed out some detail in a layout, the thickness of his lashes, when she and Marsh looked directly at one another. Rather than becoming more accustomed to his presence, she steadily grew more conscious of him.

Time flew past, and both were surprised when guests began returning from the theater. Gran was yawning behind her hand.

Vivi felt wide awake but she realized even though Marsh didn't act weary, he must be, after his long and busy day on crutches.

"I think I'll call it a day, too. A night. Whatever," she decided.

"The princess retiring to her tower?" Marsh suggested, smiling.

"Sleeping Beauty," Vivi said lightly. "Or maybe Cinderella, since tomorrow it's back to getting breakfasts and doing dishes and changing beds. Goodnight, Marsh. Grannie, sleep well. I'll see you in the morning."

Although she was stimulated, by the time Vivi climbed clear up to her circular room in the tower, her little bed with its old-fashioned quilt looked extremely welcoming. She turned it down, then carried her dainty batiste nightgown into the bath to shower and change.

Marsh's ads. They circled through her mind's eye as

90

she got ready for bed. They were excitingly fresh and innovative. She wished she had brought some of hers along to show him.

Except, she abruptly realized, she wasn't that proud of the majority. She did a good job of giving the station what it wanted, but the Continuity Director wanted hit-em-over-the-head sensationalism, with sex-related buzz words. Sophistication, he called it. Vivi didn't feel Marsh would be favorably impressed by that sort of thing.

Slipping between the cool white cotton percale sheets, Vivi automatically reached for the book she was reading and made a face when it wasn't on the bedside table. Belatedly, she remembered taking it downstairs.

"Well, I'm not going down there after it, not in my nightgown," she muttered under her breath. "It's not the greatest thing I've ever read, anyway."

She switched off the squatty brass lamp with its hobnail glass shade and snuggled down, smiling into her pillow as she recalled all the good memories of this day. She'd have pleasant dreams tonight.

But sleep of any sort eluded her. She found this infuriating. She always slept well, so why was she wakeful tonight? Overexcited? It *had* been quite a day, with the normal routine of running a bed-and-breakfast house, then chauffeuring Marsh to Terre Haute and visiting the stations there.

Yes, and Barry's letter! He must be missing her to write her this soon. Perhaps he was coming around to the realization that marriage to her would be entirely different from the disastrous relationship with his ex-wife.

Somehow, her mind angled off onto thoughts of

that party. She hated big noisy parties. Could she get out of the party Barry was planning? Surely she could, if she set her mind to it. Except then there'd always be another party and another, for Barry loved that scene and never willingly missed one.

Money. How would she manage financially once Jill moved out? Could she find a smaller, less-expensive apartment, for just herself? A studio apartment would be enough, but many of them cost almost as much.

Besides, unless she did have a roommate, Barry was going to continue to pressure her to move in with him. Where could she find a congenial person to live with, and fast? Maybe Gran's suggestion to put an ad on a church bulletin board would work. She needn't accept just any girl who answered the ad. She'd talk things over with applicants before deciding. And the fact that she met one through a church didn't mean the girl would be holier-than-thou. Neither Gran nor Marsh were. Still....

Vivi flounced over and reshaped her pillow. *Think positive thoughts, not worrisome ones,* she ordered herself. Instead, her stomach signaled a new problem: she was hungry. How could she get to sleep with her tummy grumbling?

"I am *not* going downstairs to raid the fridge," she whispered. Sneak down and turn on lights? Even if she went down the stairs, she'd be sure to disturb Marsh, and maybe some of the other guests, as well.

Pumpkin cookies. She'd bought a small bag of pumpkin cookies Saturday at the courthouse craft tent, and, with Gran's molasses hermits in the kitchen cookie jar, she'd virtually forgotten them in the meantime.

She could nibble a cookie or two now and drink a

glass of water. Read a little bit, even. That was the rec-
ommended cure for insomnia, wasn't it?

She reached for the lamp switch, blinked against the
sudden brightness, and got out of bed to hunt for the
cookies. What should she read? She hated to begin
one story before she finished another.

Vivi chuckled to herself as her eyes strayed over the
stack of books on the nightstand shelf. That Bible
which Gran had been after her to read was the very
thing! Reading all those columns of fine print on thin
paper, with archaic words—oh, that ought to put her
to sleep in no time flat, and she could truthfully tell
Gran that she had read in it.

The pumpkin cookies were good. And so was this
Bible. Vivi was surprised by both. For one thing, the
Bible looked like an ordinary book, with decent-size
print and good paper, with no distracting numbers
and italics, and with down-to-earth language. An ordinary person like herself could read it.

Vivi was surprised at how engrossing the creation
story actually was. She read on to Noah and the great
flood. With her vivid imagination, Vivi fleshed out
story after story. She'd somehow imagined the biblical
characters to be virtuous and dull, but here were exciting tales of faith and deceit, of infidelity—and of true
love. How much Jacob must have loved his Rachel, to
work so long and hard to win her as his wife, and to
continue in that love until his dying day!

Vivi read swiftly and with fascination. She finished
the cookies and Genesis and skimmed on in to Exodus. Many of these events were familiar to her from
past sermons and films, yet the brief biblical versions
seemed fresh and new. The Ten Commandments. Had

she ever really studied them? They seemed beautifully simple and practical.

Dimly, Vivi heard the mellow chime of the mantel clock as it struck the hour and half-hour far below in the living room. She should turn out her light and get some sleep. She knew she could sleep now, but fascinated, she read on.

Only when Exodus ended did Vivi firmly close the book, a slim forefinger marking her place while she searched for the silk-tasseled bookmark Gran had left in the back.

She smiled at the quote from Psalms on it: "God is our refuge and our strength, a very present help in trouble."

"God, You've given me a lovely day and evening," she murmured into the night softly illuminated by the autumn moon. "I really thank You for it. Now, please show me the way to go with my problems—Barry and a roommate. Gran says I should pray. Can You help me?"

Chapter Seven

"Hey, there, Sleeping Beauty! Forget to set your alarm clock?" Marsh hailed, as Vivi clattered down the back stairs and burst into the kitchen.

"What're you doing here?" she asked, startled to see him leaning against the range, rhythmically stirring a big skillet of scrambled eggs. "Are you trying to get my job?"

He shrugged easily, but his glance was keenly assessing. "We thought maybe you had quit or were on strike for higher wages or better working conditions."

"It isn't like you to oversleep," Gran fussed, lifting a tray of small glasses filled with orange or tomato juice and starting into the dining room. "Didn't you sleep well last night?"

"No, I slept like a baby," Vivi assured her, getting her bearings and setting to work at the toaster.

Marsh still eyed her with steady concern which seemed to probe deep inside her. "Didn't your alarm ring?"

"I don't have an alarm. Not a clock, anyway," Vivi qualified. "I always wake at dawn. Well, almost always."

He still watched and waited. "I was awake pretty late last night, and I could see light from a window that must've been your tower." He gestured outdoors. "It reflects on the house over there. Something wrong? That letter you got from the boyfriend?"

"Barry? Heavens, no. Well, maybe a little, at the beginning." Gran bustled back in, her tray now empty, and Vivi told them both, "I had trouble getting to sleep, so I thought I'd read a little while, and I began on that Bible, Gran." She made a laughingly rueful grimace. "I got hooked and couldn't put it down. I kept wondering about this and that in it, details like what Rachel looked like, and the burning bush, and manna, and what this and that looked and felt like." She shook her head firmly. "The result was that I didn't wake up on time!"

"Ah," Marsh said appreciatively. "I'll have to introduce you to my favorite Bible. It has all manner of footnotes and explanations of those very things."

"Yes, but not now, Marsh!" Gran ordered, looking alarmed. "We've got breakfast to serve, and you see how Vivi is when she gets her nose in a book! How are those eggs coming?"

"Ready to dish up," Marsh said cheerfully, turning off the burner and wrapping a potholder around the skillet handle. Carefully he lifted the pan and turned to begin spooning fluffy golden scrambled eggs out onto the waiting plates.

Link sausages already waited on those plates. Vivi added crisp hot toast, thrust more slices of bread into the toaster slots, and began carrying plates to the dining room, where the guests were finishing their juice. She offered to refill coffee cups, then hastened back into the kitchen.

They were busy for the next hour, cooking and serving the hearty breakfasts and then washing up the small mountain of dirty dishes and silverware.

Marsh insisted upon remaining to help. Vivi had initially assumed he only started to pinch-hit because she was late coming down, but he refused to leave. Once the food was all cooked and served, he edged across to the sink, filling one side with hot sudsy water and the other with steaming rinse water, and began washing the dishes as Vivi cleared them from the dining table.

"You don't have to do that. You're supposed to be a guest here," Vivi scolded.

"Aahhh—!" he scoffed, easing more juice glasses into the water. "It's the least I can do, the way you two have had to wait on me. Besides, this takes me back to my college days. I was the best dishwasher the cafeteria ever had."

Gran and Vivi exchanged amused glances. "As I said last night, he prides himself on his humility," Vivi commented.

"I told you I believe in telling the truth," Marsh protested, grinning. As Vivi brought dishes over to the counter, he reached to dab a blob of suds on the tip of her nose, his eyes gleaming provocatively.

"If you weren't on crutches—!" she threatened.

"You'd what?" he challenged. "What?"

She shook her head and wiped off her nose. "I'm not telling you, so you can be prepared! You just behave."

"If I were you, Marsh, I'd hang onto those crutches," Gran warned.

By the time the dishes were all washed and dried, the guests had left for the square and the sightseeing routes, and the house was quiet. Marsh retreated to the porch as Gran got out the vacuum cleaner, and Vivi hurried upstairs to strip and change beds in the rooms where guests had checked out.

"You two go enjoy yourselves, and I'll take care of doing the laundry," Gran commanded when Vivi brought the basket of rumpled sheets and pillowcases downstairs. "You've worked enough for one day, and I appreciate your help. Now scat!"

Vivi went out to the porch and joined Marsh. "I've been fired," she told him, as she dropped into a rocker. "Gran wants to get rid of us for the day."

"Giving you time off for good behavior, is she?" he teased. Kitticat was curled in his lap, purring as his fingers stroked her furry little body. "Decide yet which of the routes you want to take?"

Vivi shrugged. "Looks like you've been studying the map. What do you suggest?"

He glanced down at the half-open map of Parke County. "As you say, they're all good. You're the driver. I'll go wherever you take me."

"A big help you are," she grumbled as she reached for the map. "The most bridges are on the Red Route, so do we want to start with it or save the best till last?"

"If we start with the best, we'll definitely see it," he said logically. "Save it till last, and we might have hard rains and end by missing it."

"You talked me into it," Vivi concurred and stood up again. "Okay. I've got to go freshen up and change. Half an hour?"

What pleasant company he was, Vivi reflected as she climbed the stairs to her room. So many men—including Barry—wanted to make all the decisions, or at least to think that they did, and required special handling and persuasion.

Marsh treated her as an equal partner, neither catering to her nor expecting her to submit to his wishes. And that wasn't just because he was temporarily on crutches. He'd been just as considerate before he fell.

Vivi didn't waste time upstairs. Soon she was ready in a crisp pale blue oxford shirt and jeans, her hair swirled in casual elegance, discreet make-up on her eyes and lips. She raced back down the steps, eager for the day's outing. Today was autumn at its best. The air was clear with a slight nip warmed by the sun.

Marsh was navigator, with the map and a guidebook for identification folded open on his knee.

All the routes began at the square. Vivi drove carefully as they threaded through the crowded streets, following the route signs and sneaking only a quick peek at the town's oldest building. Once it had been the local jail, and executions had taken place there.

"Says here tickets were sold to people who wanted to watch," Marsh reported from the booklet. "Not exactly my idea of entertainment. Is it yours?"

"Mine? I'm so tenderhearted, I can't put down traps for mice," Vivi disclaimed.

"And coming up next, on the other side of this railroad bridge, we come to the sewage disposal plant and then the meat processing plant," Marsh continued instructively.

"Look, I'm here to see bridges, not executions and sewers and meat processors," Vivi retorted.

"How about scarecrows?" he asked with interest. There was always a scarecrow-making contest, with some good ones along the routes.

"That, too," Vivi conceded. "And nice old houses." She turned her head to smile at him. "Isn't the first bridge fairly close now?"

Three bridges did come up quite soon, one after the other, nestled among the glorious autumn hues. Big Raccoon Creek meandered among the hills, its silvery water splashing over rocks and glittering in the sun.

Vivi slowed the little red car to a crawl as they entered each bridge. With no other cars close behind them, they could take their time and study the construction.

"You know the bridges were used by courting couples," Marsh mentioned, a tantalizing gleam in his hazel eyes as he studied Vivi rather than the bridge. "A nice private spot to stop the horse and buggy for a little spooning."

"I'm sure that's why so many were built," Vivi said dryly. "Not for protection from the elements or anything so mundane!"

"I was hoping, when you slowed down—" he murmured.

"I'm just obeying the sign on the bridge. 'Cross This Bridge at a Walk,' " Vivi claimed. "Are you watching our route signs? We could wander these hills forever, otherwise."

"I'd really rather watch you, and it'd all be pretty scenery," he said comfortably. "We go straight from here to Bridgeton. Want to stop there and walk around? According to the booklet, it has quite a bit worth seeing."

"Why not?" Vivi agreed. "We have all the time in the world." She suspected his folded body might be aching from the confinement of ner little car.

Ordinarily, Bridgeton was a tiny village which made Rockville seem like a bustling city. During the Covered Bridge Festival, however, its streets were full of cars and yellow tour buses, with people walking around, exploring the bridge, the old grist mill, and the various shops and stands.

Vivi came along just as another car pulled out of a parking place right in the center of town. She helped Marsh get onto his feet and put his crutches in place, and they joined the other tourists in wandering and looking.

"Ice cream cone?" Marsh invited, noticing a stand. "Persimmon? No, we already tried that on Saturday. Hot apple? Pumpkin?"

"I had pumpkin cookies last night, up in my room," Vivi remarked. "Something tells me Genesis and pumpkin cookies will forever be connected in my mind!"

"Next time you get the urge to pig out, how about sharing with me?" His voice was plaintive, but he spoiled the pitiable effect by continuing briskly, "I know what you mean. When I smell or taste gingerbread, it takes me straight back to the first time I went snow skiing. I don't know why. I've had it plenty of times before and since."

"And songs," Vivi said. "Whenever I hear Willie Nelson's recording of 'Stardust,' I'm back hunting a parking place at Northwest Plaza. Now why that, of all silly things?"

They ordered pumpkin and hot apple ice cream cones, and sauntered on, laughing at a puppy wearing a sandwich board. One side said "Try Our Home-Fried Pies" and the other side read "Pet Me, 95¢." They looked across at the covered bridge, but decided against walking through it.

Arts and crafts were available for sale at stands and in gift and antique shops. There were a pottery shop, a quaint old country store, art studios, and a bank once robbed by John Dillinger.

Since the ice cream only whetted their appetites, they stopped at another place for sandwiches of country ham on homemade bread.

"Tomorrow..." Marsh said contemplatively. "Tomorrow, how about throwing together a picnic lunch and eating at Turkey Run? That's up on the Blue Route. Actually, I'd planned on renting a canoe up there and floating down Sugar Creek while I was here this time, but with this ankle I'd be a menace in a boat. And I don't think these crutches would make particularly good paddles."

"Next time you come," Vivi consoled. "Yes, why not? I think a picnic would be fun."

"It's a date, then," Marsh said comfortably, smiling down at her. "Hey, look at these duck decoys. Isn't this one a beauty? Looks so real. you can hear him quack!"

"Sounds like an old-fashioned outing to me," Gran said, bright-eyed with interest. "What do you plan to take?"

"I hadn't thought that far yet," Vivi admitted. "Common sense says to keep it simple, and yet..." Why on earth should she want to show off a little, impress Marsh with what a delectable meal she could spread?

Gran's glance was femininely knowing. "No need to throw together baloney sandwiches and potato chips. There's a cut-up frying chicken in the freezer, if you want to fix it. Fried chicken's as good cold as hot."

"And potato salad..." Vivi murmured thoughtfully. People always commented favorably on her potato salad.

"Then you could make a fresh vegetable salad with the last of those little tomatoes," Gran suggested. "There's green pepper and broccoli you could chop into it. I like a little cauliflower, too, for color contrast."

"And cider," Vivi concluded. "It's so good and fresh now, isn't it?"

"Just as long as you don't get hard cider by mistake," Gran commented. "Now that could cause you problems!"

Laughing in agreement, Vivi went into the kitchen to survey the food and begin pulling items out of the refrigerator and freezer. Salads were better if they had time to sit and season, so she might as well begin now. The chicken could thaw overnight and be ready to cook in the morning. This would make enough to leave some at home for Gran's lunch, as well. In fact, Gran may have had that in mind when she helped plan the menu.

"This is supposed to be the prettiest route," Marsh commented as they stowed the picnic basket in the back of the car and set out. "Not as popular as some, though." He grinned. "It doesn't have as many bridges—or craft and antique shops."

For the first few miles they traveled north on Route 41, and then they branched off onto a side road, to wend their way on into Turkey Run State Park.

"It may not have as many shops and bridges, but it also doesn't have as much traffic," Vivi said lightly. "That makes it nice for us."

"Yes, from the looks of things today, we won't have people horning in on our picnic."

Vivi gave him a smiling glance of agreement. She

didn't begrudge the other sightseers, but it was pleasant to have extra space and more privacy to eat and talk and gaze at the lovely scenery.

For all her initial reluctance, when Marsh had joined her last Saturday, she enjoyed sightseeing more with him as a companion. He'd turned into a congenial and undemanding friend with whom she could relax. Vivi was almost startled to realize how recently they'd met. She felt as if she'd known him always.

They stopped at the Cherokee Trading Post to inspect the curiosity shop, antiques, and crafts offered there. Apple butter, candy, smoked hams, and both apple and cherry cider were sold as well.

"Good. Gran told me to wait and get it here," Vivi said. "What kind do you want? Apple or cherry?"

"I'm a man for traditional things," Marsh said. "In the autumn, apple cider."

Driving on, they passed the canoe rental signs. Marsh turned his head to study them, and Vivi felt regret for him. It was disappointing to look forward to something and then be prevented from doing it.

"Another time," he commented philosophically. "It isn't a now-or-never thing. I know I'm coming back here. Probably often."

"Of course." She wondered whether they'd meet again if he did. He'd probably stay with Gran again, as he had before. However, would she be here? How would things be with Barry by then?

"We might investigate the Narrows Bridge area for our picnic," Marsh mentioned, a little farther on. "As I remember, it's a great spot for one."

They reached the bridge in only a few minutes more, and they were in luck. Ample parking space was available at the roadside, and only a few other people were walking about.

Vivi helped Marsh out, then stood, head lifted, gazing around. Marsh was right; this was a gorgeous spot. Sugar Creek narrowed to run between sandstone cliffs at this point, with trees spilling over the clifftops. The low bluffs descended in broad natural stairsteps in places and gave easy access to the water.

"Do people fish here?" she wanted to know. "It looks like an ideal spot for it. And for canoeing. I never have been in a canoe, but seeing this place makes me want to."

"Next time," he promised, smiling down at her. "Maybe next year we'll come back. Our annual picnic at the Narrows? Only next time we'll leave the car back where we rent the canoe and come downstream by boat."

"Maybe," Vivi said, willing to make believe with him. They wouldn't, of course. Still, it was a pleasant fantasy, harming no one. Maybe it would happen. If they both returned, it would be an agreeable way to spend a few hours.

"Now," Marsh announced. "Let's find a place to have the picnic. That basket isn't too heavy, is it? I wish I could be more help carrying it."

"I'm fine," Vivi promised him. "It isn't really heavy, though mind you, I don't want to take it on any long hike. Where are we going to have our picnic? You evidently know this terrain better than I do."

"We might try going along the creek a little way," Marsh suggested, taking the lead and surveying the banks on either side. "Over along here, maybe?"

"Can you manage that with your crutches?" The sandstone made several broad shallow steps from the road down toward the path which ran along beside the creek.

"Sure. Just like the porch steps back at the house." His smile was reassuring. "Anyhow, I can use my foot a little bit now. Enough to get down these steps. These crutches are mainly just insurance, to make sure I don't overdo."

"If you're sure," Vivi consented, hovering as he carefully made his way down. When he reached the bottom, he turned to watch as she descended.

Soon they found the perfect spot, a grassy sun trap with a tranquil view of trees, river, and bridge. Vivi set down the basket, took out the old blanket folded in it, and spread that on the turf. Getting Marsh down onto it was a major undertaking, and she suspected that getting him back up onto his feet would be even more of a job, but somehow they'd manage.

"What's to eat?" he demanded hungrily, hazel eyes intent. "I smelled it cooking and almost came in to raid the place then. Hey—that looks good."

Laughing and swatting his hands away, Vivi unpacked the chicken, the plastic containers of potato salad and garden vegetable salad, crusty rolls, cheese, and half an apple pie. Gran had several pies in the freezer, and they'd thawed and baked one this morning. It still felt faintly warm to the touch.

"Oh, Gran's famous for her apple pies," Vivi declared. "I'll have to get her to give me a lesson. She makes them from scratch, no written recipe, just a pinch of this and a chunk of that, and they all turn out delicious. You'll see."

"Can we start with the dessert and finish with the chicken and salads?" Marsh asked hopefully. And Vivi wasn't sure he was just joking.

They ate lazily, soaking up the October sunshine, watching the stream, the birds, and the tourists who were sometimes visible up at the bridge, and wishing that a deer might appear. Idly they talked and enjoyed the delectable food. In their interested exchange of ideas, sometimes they spoke with full mouths, too at ease with one another to bother with formal manners.

After finishing the food, Marsh stretched out on his back, squinting up at the sky, and Vivi tidily packed away their leftovers and the emptied containers. Then she lounged on an elbow, alternately watching his expressive face and the sky as he indicated various clouds.

"Look at that one—it looks like your grandmother's house."

"It looks like whipped cream to me," Vivi amiably differed.

"Don't you ever think of anything but food? Look at it. There's the porch. There's your tower."

"Modeled in whipped cream," Vivi maintained.

He had such good bone structure. And the lines in his face, around his eyes, and that strong mouth were those of good humor and tenderness. He was tanned, but just to the right degree, not like someone who made a narcissistic project of acquiring the world's most perfect tan. He was much more worth watching than puffy white clouds.

The sun shifted, and the trees dappled them with shade, flickering as the breeze moved the branches. Before long, their little picnic paradise would be completely in shade and too cool for comfort.

"Maybe we should get going," Marsh spoke, echoing her thoughts. His hand sketched a gesture at the clouds. "All we're getting are woolly lambs now, and you know what counting sheep leads to."

"Definitely," Vivi said, and rolled onto her knees. She got to her feet and reached down her hands to grasp his. "Are you ready? Then—up!"

He surged to his feet, overbalanced slightly, and clung to her to steady himself. His hazel eyes, above hers yet so near, were full of laughter. Had he really overbalanced, or was he merely faking it, knowing she'd grab and hold him to provide stability till he found his own?

"Have a crutch," she said dryly, "and behave yourself. I have to carry the basket."

She thrust his crutches at him, then busied herself shaking leaves and grass off the blanket, folding it into a neat square, and fitting it back into the picnic basket.

Although Marsh favored his injured ankle, he was able to put weight on it, Vivi noticed as they climbed back up to the road. She had had moments of fearing he might have injured it worse than they'd first thought and wouldn't be able to drive his Corvette when he was ready to leave Rockville.

"Leave the basket in the car, and let's walk across the bridge," Marsh proposed as they reached where the little red car sat parked. "I'd like a really good look at the interior of the bridge, wouldn't you?"

"Yes, we really don't get a good enough look, driving through," Vivi consented. "Even if we stopped, we wouldn't."

So they strolled on along the dusty road, out of the sunshine into the cool shadowy tunnel of the bridge, her footsteps and his crutches resounding hollowly on the strong plank floor. This was a long bridge, with several windows cut in its sides to provide light and a view.

They paused at one window to peer out at the water and the formation of the sandstone cliffs and to try to locate the spot where they had picnicked.

"It might have been any of those outcroppings," Vivi eventually commented. "From here they all look so much alike."

"Next time we'll fasten a white flag there so we'll know," Marsh said. "Or you can stand there in your red shirt, and I'll come back up here and take a picture to commemorate it."

"Do you really suppose there'll be a next time?" Vivi asked, half wistfully. "I'm not even sure I want there to be. Today has been so good, coming back could be anticlimactic."

"Or even better," Marsh suggested, voice soft and caressing. "Yes, I think there will be a next time. Maybe several next times—an annual event—and they'll get better and better." He grinned at her, tone and expression shifting from intimate to teasing. "For one thing, next time I'll carry that basket!"

"I don't have to be the one on crutches, do I?" Vivi demanded with mock-alarm.

"No, if you can't walk on your own two feet, I'll carry you," he promised. "Piggyback!"

Chuckling together, they walked on to the far end of the bridge, waited while a car passed, then turned to saunter back. Vivi supposed that when they got to their starting point, they would get in the car, drive the rest of the Blue Route, and return to Gran's. She didn't want to. This had been such a quietly magical day, she didn't want it to end. But it had to. She knew that.

Again they paused at a window to gaze out at the opposite reaches of Sugar Creek. The sun glittered blindingly on the greenish water of the stream, and birds

109

called. All the ordinary small sounds seemed distinct in the wooded hush.

"You know," Marsh murmured contemplatively, "there were several uses for these bridges. Year-round mistletoe, for one. It was traditional for couples to kiss whenever they crossed through a covered bridge. And we've already established that we both like old, traditional things, haven't we?"

"Year-round mistletoe?" Vivi questioned, laughing up at him. "I wonder why I've never heard that before? That couples did court in them, yes, but that they were supposed to? How many bridges have we been through before this one?"

"But then we were in the car," Marsh pointed out, balancing on his good right foot as he removed his crutches and leaned them against the side of the bridge. "I don't believe in distracting the driver. But now—"

Strong gentle hands reached to draw her close, and his head bent, his lips searching for hers. His eyes were intent, holding her gaze and mesmerizing her.

"Marsh—" she breathed, as his arms came about her.

"You'd better put your arms around me, too, to make sure I don't fall," he murmured, feathering kisses all around her delicately formed ear, then trailing them on across to claim her mouth.

She tightened her embrace—to steady him—at first, at least. The sensation surprised her. She'd never liked kissing a very tall man, but Marsh felt so right, strong and solid.

The teasing kiss which started out as casually as any mistletoe salute, with both of them laughing, abruptly

110

intensified and escalated into something startling in its impact.

Vivi drew back, her brown eyes huge and questioning as they gazed up into his.

"Hey," he breathed. "There's a lot to be said for tradition, isn't there?"

Chapter Eight

"Do you suppose it's going to rain today?" Vivi peered out the kitchen alcove's windows. "That would certainly put a damper on the festival." She grimaced ruefully. "Sorry about the pun!"

"I hope not." Gran had extra reason to hope not. On a rainy day, guests were more inclined to stay in the house, grumbling and unhappy, or to track in mud. "It's early yet. We often have a little shower about dawn; then it clears by the time breakfast is over."

"Let's hope." Vivi felt reluctant to spend the day indoors, in Marsh's company. "Well, let's get this show on the road. Scrambled eggs again?"

Briskly they began preparing the usual hearty breakfasts. Vivi welcomed the activity. Without it, her thoughts roved back, dwelling on that embrace on the bridge. So unexpectedly pleasant—stirring—yet how could it be? When she had Barry, how could she have allowed another man to kiss her, even in jest, far less enjoyed it so much?

"Don't kill those eggs," Gran tartly advised, as Vivi beat them preparatory to pouring them into the hot skillet. "Mercy! Did you get up on the wrong side of the bed this morning?"

"Could be," Vivi granted. "But better to take it out on the eggs than anything else, right?"

"It's not just because we've got an overcast morning?" Gran probed. "Do you have other problems, maybe?" She poured orange juice into the small glasses lined up on the table. "Now when I've got a troubled mind, that's when I turn to the Bible. Sometimes you just open it at random, and it's like it's speaking to you, the way your eyes fall on words that just fit your situation. You might try that." She smiled, eyes crinkling and twinkling. "But not till breakfast's over. I need you here, not buried in the book!"

Vivi laughed, reluctantly but genuinely. "No, no, I promise, we'll get all the chores done before I read anything at all."

She had read more from the Bible last night at bedtime and first thing this morning, when she always did read a little, but she hadn't encountered anything which seemed to apply to her own life. The interesting stories had helped to distract her, but they were not particularly relevant to her needs.

Determinedly, Vivi continued scrambling eggs and frying bacon. She was relieved nobody asked for pancakes, Happy Face or otherwise, for just doing bacon and eggs kept both Gran and her quite busy enough. It wasn't as much fun without Marsh to help them, but his assistance yesterday had only been due to the fact that she'd overslept.

She had the routine clearing up and household chores to help with before she was free to go up to her own room for a bath and to change before starting on the next sightseeing drive.

Skies were still gray. The radio weatherman predicted scattered showers, but probable clearing by evening.

Bathing and dressing, Vivi thought wryly that she wasn't accomplishing much in the way of figuring out solutions to her everyday problems. In fact, she'd added on the problem of Marsh. How could she have responded to him?

Buttoning her blue and white plaid shirt, Vivi stopped dead, as realization struck her.

She'd met Marsh as a test of her love for Barry. That was it! Of course! A really attractive man, a friend who appealed to her physically. If she could withstand him, her love for Barry was solid and strong enough to rise above any future temptations.

Relieved to figure that out, she resumed buttoning with her slim fingers. She pulled a bibbed denim jumper on over her head, adjusted its straps, and fastened the copper snaps at the waist. She slipped her feet into denim espadrilles and gave her hair a flick with the comb, then caught up her purse and hurried downstairs.

As usual, Marsh was waiting for her, though this morning he lounged in the living room with Kitticat in his lap, not out on the porch. The morning was cool as well as gloomy.

"How about the little Brown Route?" he suggested, as they started outside. "Then if it starts raining, we won't have so far to come back."

"Suits me," she assented. "There's just it and the Yellow Route left, and the Yellow Route's the longest one, isn't it?"

"And supposedly the one with the best food. That ought to be of interest to you," he teased her affectionately. "So we save it till tomorrow, in hopes the weather will be better then?"

The Brown Route was the shortest, with the fewest bridges, but the scenery was just as lovely—or would have been, if the sun had been shining. Even on a dark day, the rolling hills covered with brilliant foliage did their best to compensate, to garner any stray sunbeams.

Light rain dotted the windshield as they reached Montezuma, on the bank of the Wabash River. They peered at the pig roast and the tent full of craft exhibits, but decided against getting out to walk around.

"Not when the rain may get heavier," Marsh commented. "We can come back tomorrow or over the weekend, if we want to."

The sightseeing route turned south, past the old Wabash and Erie Canal. The narrow country road twisted and curved through the cornfields and woods and crossed two covered bridges in close succession. The windshield wipers swished back and forth in hypnotic rhythm.

The windows closed against the rain made the car too intimate a setting for Vivi's comfort. She wasn't sure how or why. It hadn't felt that way before. She wished they'd delayed this drive until tomorrow. Next best was wishing for an interesting spot where they could get out and walk around, rain or no rain. Driving at this snail's pace, it was going to take ages to get back to Gran's. The glance she'd sneaked at the map showed they were barely halfway along the route.

If only...if only...! And was wishing, hoping, a form of prayer? An informal prayer, but its meaning understood all the same?

The wipers squeaked against the glass as the rain

stopped. Vivi switched them off, feeling startled.

Marsh had been quiet, leaning back and skimming through the guidebook. "Mecca's coming up," he remarked. "Would you believe, it used to have six coal mines and a clay pipe factory—and anywhere from fourteen to fifty-six saloons? I'm not sure whether it's gone downhill or improved since those days!"

Now Vivi was tranquil enough and they had a good opportunity to get out and stroll around. Besides the usual craft shop, there was an old-fashioned one-roomed schoolhouse. The guidebook said that it was in session during the festival, but today the school was idle.

Even so, it was interesting to sit at the quaint desks and peer at the faded photographs and yellowed clippings on the walls, before going back outdoors to inspect the Mecca Bridge. This bridge was closed to traffic, but some other tourists were walking across it to take a close look at its construction and shake their heads over the graffiti.

Vivi was glad to have other people around, to diffuse the growing sense of intimacy with Marsh. Remembering their kiss yesterday at the Narrows Bridge, she would have hesitated to enter this one with him, but since two other couples were there....

"Cross this bridge at a walk," Marsh read the usual sign painted above the bridge's entrance. "A *slow* walk," he added wryly, with an expressive glance down at his crutches.

"Nonsense, you're getting around just fine," Vivi retorted. "I'm not running any races with you!"

To her dismay, when the other people reached the far end of the bridge, they kept on walking, got into a car parked there, and drove away! Why hadn't she noticed that they were on their return trip, rather than just entering as she and Marsh were?

"How considerate of them," Marsh observed appreciatively. "It isn't that I'm ashamed to be seen carrying on old customs, but part of this one is privacy—isn't it?"

Vivi lifted her head to utter a firm protest, but as she parted her lips to speak, they were claimed by Marsh's. She knew he must think she was responding to his kiss, welcoming it. Thrills ran throughout her slim body before, with an effort, she stepped away from him.

"I'd better make a mental note to avoid bridges with you," she said with an attempt at lightness. "I think we've carried on quite enough old traditions!"

"You do? I'm getting really fond of the old way of doing things—and thinking of a few brand-new traditions we might try to start." His hazel eyes had a tantalizing gleam. "We still have the Yellow Route to do tomorrow, don't forget."

"By car," Vivi said firmly. "I feel safer at the wheel, when you're around. Speaking of which, we'd better get back in mine. Look, the rain's catching up with us. We don't want to get drenched for the drive back to Gran's. You don't need a cold to go with your sprained ankle."

"Whatever you say," he agreed with a deceptive meekness that didn't match the mischief in his eyes.

According to the map, there weren't any more bridges on Route 41 between Mecca and Rockville, so Vivi drove faster. They ran out of the rain once more, but Vivi suspected it was following them.

"I meant to take you to lunch somewhere," Marsh said, as she headed for Gran's street. "In one of the towns, or somewhere here in Rockville. Not out in the open square. We could go have pizza. There are some places up on 41."

Vivi shook her head. "I'd rather go home and fix something. It might be pouring rain when we finished eating at a restaurant, and however good you are on your crutches, climbing steps and getting in and out of the car still go slow."

"I'll literally give you a rain check, then," he conceded. "Anyhow, I like your cooking, lady."

Gran's kitchen was a bright and cozy shelter from a rainy day, and Gran was happy to have them back. She was just beginning to prepare her own lunch and cheerily relinquished that job when Vivi offered to take over.

"I'll be glad of your company," she admitted, settling in her high-backed rocker.

Not half as glad as I am of yours, Vivi thought, peering into the refrigerator and then the freezer to see what was available. For once in her life, she welcomed a chaperone. Marshall William Henderson was dangerously attractive, hazardously congenial.

"How about hamburgers and fries?" he suggested, coming to look in over her shoulder, and spotting the patted-out ground beef, buns, and a plastic bag of potato sticks. "I tell you what. You've been doing enough cooking around here. Let me play chef."

"All the great chefs of the world are men, you know," Vivi confided to Gran. "I wanted to say that before he did!"

"So? It's true," he countered, unruffled. "You two set the table. I'll do the rest."

"I hate to admit it, but he may have been right about the great chefs," Vivi murmured to Gran as they shared the "great American meal." "Marsh, I never before met anyone who could raise cheeseburgers and French fries to gourmet heights!"

He grinned. "Practice! Staple fare for a bachelor. And I worked in various fast-food places, summer vacations during my college years, so I got lots of experience timing precisely how long they should fry."

Eating together at the round table in the bay window was cozy. Rain spattered against the panes, emphasizing the snug warmth of the kitchen. From time to time they heard guests enter or leave by the big front door, but no one came to ask for anything.

By the time they finished eating and the dishes were washed and put away, Gran was yawning gently. "If you young folks will excuse me, I'm going to go take a nap," she declared.

Vivi shot a suspicious glance at her. More of her grandmother's matchmaking? But Vivi knew Gran did take a nap every afternoon she could. And there was something about rainy days which made napping extremely tempting. Usually. This afternoon she felt unusually stimulated, wide awake.

"Well," Marsh drawled thoughtfully, as they watched Gran head upstairs, "any objection to my doing a little typing in here? It won't bother you? In fact, you want to help?"

"Typewriter duets?" Vivi queried skeptically, cocking her head to one side. "Now that's a new one to me."

He grinned and shook his head. "This looks to me like a good time to do a little work on that ad campaign Steve told me about. If I get it out of the way, or at least started, I won't have to spend so much time on it once I get back to the office."

119

"You've got a good day for it," Vivi said wryly, with a glance at the streaming windows. "Sure. Go ahead. But surely you aren't serious about my helping? What do I know about writing Christian advertising?"

"What did I know, when I started?" he asked in turn. "Come on. Keep me company."

"Well...why not?" Vivi consented. It would be interesting to see how Marsh worked.

In minutes, the table in the bay window became an advertising office. Marsh brought out an ultra-light electronic typewriter. She couldn't help noticing his was considerably easier to read than Barry's, and it operated silently. His attaché case was open on an adjacent chair, with typing paper, a lined yellow pad, and notes and promotional brochures about the client spread out on the table top.

Time sped past as they played with ideas, bouncing concepts off one another, occasionally typing out a page of copy to see how it looked in black and white.

Marsh was good! She'd known he was, of course, after seeing his finished radio and TV spots and the magazine pages, but she hadn't known how much time and effort and polishing might have been required to develop them.

Now she could see how swiftly he could work once the idea germinated and how incisively he thought. She eyed him with growing respect.

And he viewed her with equal admiration. She deserved it. Vivi was stimulated by his conceptions; she felt a rush of creativity. She knew she had never written better, had never been more bursting with ideas. She enjoyed showing off for him, proving to him that she could do more than make breakfasts and change beds and drive competently.

"Hey, lady, you're some writer," he praised. "Did I happen to mention that when Steve called, he said one of our writers is leaving? How about your taking her place? It would save me the hassle of interviewing a bunch of people who don't have the faintest idea what it's all about."

"Not even for that," Vivi firmly declined. "In Paducah? I like that name, and this is interesting, but remember, I live in St. Louis? That would be a pretty long commute."

She didn't mention Barry. Marsh wouldn't be impressed by that reason. Her leaving Barry behind, she suspected, was one of Marsh's prime reasons for the offer—except he wasn't serious.

Of course, Marsh wasn't serious. This was one of those offers she was expected to know as all fun. She almost wished it wasn't and that it was from a St. Louis firm.

"So relocate," he suggested. "It'd solve your housing problem. There're plenty of apartments for rent in Paducah, and they're bound to be less expensive than comparable apartments in St. Louis. What're you paying now? And what are you making where you work? We'll match it, if we can. Maybe even do better."

Was he serious? He certainly looked and sounded as if he might be. All the same...

"Thanks, but I'm happy where I am," she smilingly refused.

His eyes were keen. "Are you? I get the impression you find your situation there—well, not quite congenial."

Vivi shook her head. "I'm an adult. I don't expect perfection. For the most part, I'm quite happy. Look," she motioned outdoors, changing the subject. "When did it stop raining?"

His glance was almost too understanding, but he went along with the change. "Looks like the sun's even trying to shine. Great timing—at sundown! Better late than never, I suppose. I guess I'd better clear off this table before your grandmother needs it again."

"I'll take your attaché case and typewriter back to your room."

Anxious to escape, to have some time alone up in her room, she assisted in clearing up and wondered how to occupy the long evening. Gran wasn't the best of chaperones; she made it seem like such a cozy family gathering, and she persisted in viewing Marsh as Vivi's boyfriend, not merely another festival guest.

"We've been in the whole afternoon," Marsh mentioned, as he snapped the catch on his attaché case. "Let's go out tonight. This is one of the evenings the old-time melodrama's on at the Ritz, isn't it? Go with me."

"Oh, I don't know...." Vivi demurred.

"I can't go without you," he pointed out, with a quizzical glance down at the crutches. "You want to go. You know you do. And I owe you. Those were some dynamite ideas you threw my way."

"Well...why not?" Vivi gave in. "I think a celebration is in order, and you're right. I did intend to go." Attending a play all alone was no fun. And with other people around she wouldn't be alone with him.

After dinner, they got in her car and drove to the yellow brick theater just off the square. It seemed almost designed for people on crutches, with extra-wide spacing between the rows of seats. The house wasn't packed, and they had no trouble getting tickets or finding seats in the middle of a row, where people wouldn't need to edge past and stumble over Marsh's long legs and crutches.

"At last, a theater that fits me," he said, grinning, as they settled to wait till the olive-green curtain went up.

"It used to be an opera house, and high school graduations were held on the stage before the new high school was built," Vivi said. Of all the inane remarks. Why did she suddenly feel shy, as if she had to make conversation?

She was relieved when the play began. *Egad, the Woman in White* was intentionally terrible, a parody on turn-of-the-century dramas, complete with beautiful, innocent heroine, noble drawing-master hero, black-hearted villains, impertinent servants, abandoned wife, and, of course, the mysterious woman in white.

The audience participated with enthusiasm, cheering the hero, shouting advice and encouragement to the fair young heroine, and hissing and booing the villain. When the villain complained that he didn't have a penny to his name, a shower of coins rained onto the stage.

"Great stuff, hmm?" Marsh queried, during the intermission. "Was that you I heard booing so loud?"

"Was that you I heard whistling through his teeth?" Vivi laughed back. "Isn't this play *awful?*"

"Bet you don't have anything like it in St. Louis." He frowned at her. "Why do you want to stay in a city so lacking in amenities—! No wonder you came to Rockville."

"I love it," she agreed. "Oh, good, here we go again."

The lights dimmed and the second act began. Now

the heroine was drugged and locked in a madhouse, unsure of her own sanity, and rescued by the hero and various eccentrics. Vivi shuddered and gasped, entering into the spirit of the performance, clutching at Marsh's hand when it comfortingly covered hers.

"You can let go now," she murmured between scenes, lifting her hand.

"Why?" he said blandly, retaining her hand and starting to play with her fingers. "You may need to be comforted again!"

With him holding her hand, this began to feel uncomfortably like a date. True, they were in a crowded theater, but it was dark, and his fingers drew tantalizing designs on the back of her hand.

Vivi was relieved when the play came to a rousing conclusion, and Marsh released her hand to join in the thunderous applause. The cast took curtain call after curtain call, beaming and bowing.

"Oh, I loved it! I loved it!" Vivi sighed, as they left the Ritz with the rest of the audience. Everyone was cheerful, chuckling over the exaggerated "mellerdrammer."

"Glad you came?" His tone and glance seemed to be asking far more than the simple question.

"I'm very glad you asked me," Vivi assured him. "You know, this has been a wonderful day, rain or no rain."

"Sure has." He grinned ruefully. "And you know what? I'm hungry again. Do you suppose any of those cookies are left?"

When they got back to the big old white Victorian house, they tiptoed in, whispering and laughing softly. Gran always left a dim light on in the hallway. Marsh's crutches were rubber-tipped, and under his expert handling they made less sound than Vivi's heels.

In the kitchen, she turned on only the soft lamp above the breakfast table before she poured milk into glasses, then got the cookie jar. It still contained a good supply of fat, raisin-studded molasses hermits.

Quietly they talked of the play and their sightseeing as they snacked on cookies and milk. Their low voices, the dim lighting, and the otherwise silence of the house created an atmosphere of intimacy. They spoke less and less, and their eyes met, clung. Vivi was intensely aware of him. She felt as if she were magnetically drawn to him. She could resist the pull, but she remained conscious of it.

Vivi rose to put the lid back on the cookie jar. She rinsed their glasses in cold water and set them in the sink. And she wasn't surprised when she turned from the sink to find she'd pivoted into Marsh's arms.

His head bent to hers, slowly, his big hands on her waist with a firm yet gentle grip, steadying her rather than restraining her. If she chose to pull away, she had the time, the freedom, before his lips descended to her mouth.

And she couldn't. She knew she should reject him, should break loose, and she absolutely couldn't. His mouth was possessive as it covered hers. His hands tightened as he drew her into a close embrace. He held her as if she were very precious and yet all woman, to love rather than to idolize from afar.

The hands she raised to push against his chest instead slid up to curve about his shoulders and then to ruffle the short hair at his nape. Her eyes closed, her lashes like tiny dark fans against her cheeks.

Only when his lips left hers, when his faintly rough jaw rubbed against the silken skin of hers, did Vivi summon strength to draw back.

"I—Marsh—I hope you won't think I'm a tease or anything like that, but—we mustn't. Please don't kiss me again. Tonight. Or tomorrow. Please," she appealed.

He studied her, frowning slightly, yet he wasn't angry. "You liked it," he pointed out. "Vivi, you're as drawn to me as I am to you. Neither of us can deny that. It's dishonest even to try."

"Yes, but—" She bit her lip, and her gesture pleaded for understanding. "If your faith is more than lip service, you know it isn't right. Not when I'm committed to Barry."

His eyes were steady on hers. "Much more than lip service," he confirmed. "But where Barry's concerned—are you sure about him? From things you've mentioned about your station personnel and the parties, you're far more suited to me. I wouldn't pursue you if I really believed, down deep, that you and he are right for one another."

"You don't want to believe it," Vivi murmured, and shook her head despairingly. "I don't know. Right now I'm so mixed up, I couldn't swear to anything. But I do know that until I see Barry again and know definitely, I'm going to try to be true to him. I can't be any other way, Marsh."

He surveyed her, his face somber. Finally he nodded. "Then you'd better get up to bed and beyond my reach. Knowing what's the right thing—the ethical and sensible thing—somehow doesn't help much when you're close enough to touch." He smiled slightly. "It's a good thing you're up on the third floor and I've got this ankle slowing me down."

Vivi's faint smile echoed his. "You're telling me? I'm

having the same problem. So…goodnight. I'll see you at breakfast."

"Go on," he told her. "I'll get the light."

Vivi hurried out of the kitchen, bending to slip off her shoes and carry them in her left hand as she ran up the stairs. She didn't want to disturb any of their guests. She didn't want to see anyone right now.

In her round tower room, she closed her door and stood, hands pressed against her hot face. She'd supposed that she'd be able to solve her problems by coming to stay with Gran for the few days of the festival. How could she have ever guessed that she'd add an even larger one to their number?

Her eyes fell upon the Bible on the nightstand by her bed. The blue silk tassel of the bookmark reminded her of the Psalms quotation on it: "God is our refuge and our strength, a very present help in trouble."

"That's what I need right now," she said under her breath. "A refuge and a source of strength, a present help to solve these troubles of mine. It's really beyond me to figure out what to do!"

Chapter Nine

"How can it be Friday already?" Vivi peered out the window of her tower aerie as if expecting to find some answer in the treetops outside.

Not only was the week ending, but autumn as well. When she'd arrived a week ago, the red-gold leaves on this big maple had been so thick she could hardly see the street below. Now they were so thin she had a good view, and they carpeted the lawn beneath the branches.

Today. Tomorrow. Sunday. Then she'd pack up her plastic shopping bags and get back into her little red car—alone—for the two-hundred-mile drive home. She'd say good-bye to Gran. To Marsh. Would she ever see either of them again? The future was uncertain enough for young people, and Gran was old.

She wasn't ready to leave here. She loved this town, this house, the peaceful tenor of life, the comfortable old kitchen with so much space to spread out and cook, the table in the bay window, the rocker, and the basket chair.

Her eyes fell upon the book on the nightstand. She hadn't finished reading Gran's new Bible yet. Smiling, she shook her head. That was the very least of her problems. Gran would be delighted to loan it to her, probably would even give it to her.

Firmly, Vivi attempted to turn her mind to brighter channels. She'd be glad to get home to her own attractive apartment again. Of course she would. Maybe its kitchen was designed for midgets who hated to cook, but the bedroom was twice the size of this tower room, with plenty of closet space and a gleaming modern bathroom.

Would Barry call her? He knew when she was due back. Maybe she could call him, to tell him she'd gotten in, and he could bring her up to date about happenings at the television station.

Why didn't she feel more enthusiastic? She liked her job. Oh, some of the people were less than perfect soul mates, and advertising did suggest sexual overtones—buy this, do that, to be more enticing to the opposite sex—but that was life. She couldn't change the world.

But brainstorming with Marsh yesterday afternoon had been—well—*uplifting*. She'd felt—oh, *inspired* seemed an exaggeration. They'd had fun. Learning to write a new type of advertising had been challenging.

He had to have been joking when he offered her a job. How could she go so much farther from home, from Barry, gamble on the unknown? It was unthinkable.

And what was she doing, standing up here, her mind wandering, while Marsh waited below for them to start on their sightseeing jaunt? The last of the routes, the last day together. Oh, the weekend lay ahead, but they probably wouldn't be out in the car, just the two of them, alone together again.

They were starting later today. The Yellow Route was known for its good food, particularly the pit-roasted beef and homemade pies at Tangier, so they were neatly planning their arrival to coincide with lunchtime.

Marsh was watching a television game show in the living room when she came downstairs. The show was virtually over, and she sat down on the arm of the sofa to watch—just until they saw whether the contestant won the grand prize.

Marsh rose far more easily today and carried his crutches rather than using them, although he favored his left ankle. He nodded down toward it. "By Sunday I should be functioning normally. I'd rather go to church without those things."

"Bring them along today—just in case," Vivi directed. "You don't want to overdo just because you feel better."

"Right. Shall we get along?"

Everything seemed so normal between them, Vivi could hardly believe last night had happened. Had they really embraced in the late-night hush of the dimly lit kitchen? Had he actually said—? And had *she*—?

This morning they were friends again, casually at ease with one another. Vivi felt that she could tell him anything, that she could be herself, with the knowledge that he would understand.

The Yellow Route left Rockville by the same road that the Brown Route did, but the sunshine today made the scenery glow with greater beauty. One of the yellow school buses which served as a tour bus was up ahead perhaps a quarter of a mile. Vivi could keep it in sight and relax about the route markers.

"So," Marsh said, "you keep an eye on your own station's output at work. What do you watch for your own pleasure?"

"Oh, all sorts of things. Actually, I like to read more than I like watching TV. Aside from some of the things on PBS, it all seems to be car chases and violence, and the comedy's nothing but one-liner put-downs. What do you watch?"

"News and sports, mostly. Some documentaries. I guess I'm like you. I'd rather read or listen to my stereo than watch most of what's on the tube."

Vivi nodded, considering his words. She could tell him anything. Barry teased her because she disliked the music shows where the dancers' costumes and movements were suggestive and comedies which hinged upon smutty behavior. If that made her prudish, then maybe she was. However, Marsh was obviously knowledgeable and sophisticated, so if he felt the same way, she couldn't be hopelessly square.

As they drove, they idly discussed what they read. He liked adventure and history and nonfiction, whereas Vivi preferred women's magazines on cooking and homemaking and light escape novels. By the end of a day of realism, she needed a few minutes' escape into a world where people still believed in marriage and babies and mutual and ethical considerations.

The big blue community building in Tangier was crowded with bus tourists standing in line for their pit-roast beef dinners. Vivi and Marsh joined the serving line, got plates and beverages, then found seats at a table, taking their time and talking as they ate.

The bus tours gave their passengers only half an hour to stop, eat, and shop in the adjacent farmers' market, so soon the building was virtually deserted. Vivi and Marsh could sit on, without feeling guilty over monopolizing this table.

Later, they browsed freely along the market displays. The majority of the goods offered for sale were the same from town to town and duplicated what was in the big tent on the Rockville square: jams and jellies, fancy breads, candies, crocheted and quilted items, and paintings.

Here however, an elderly gentleman was demonstrating musical instruments he had made. Melon-shaped dulcimers hung on a display board at the back of his booth. He had others on a stand in front of him and cheerfully told about his crafts.

"Sit down. Try playing it yourself," he urged them, with a twinkle in his eyes. "Try playing this one. It's a double dulcimer. Courting couples used to play them, alone in the parlor. As long as the girl's father could hear both of them playing, he left them alone, but if they fell silent for more than a minute or two, he was right in there to check up."

"Bridges *and* dulcimers?" Vivi murmured, with a teasing glance up at Marsh, as she sat down and fingered the strings.

Although she had never before seen a dulcimer, she had learned a few chords for a folk guitar, and all stringed instruments were basically the same. With one hand she fingered the strings to change the notes, while she plucked with the other.

Playing duets on a dulcimer was an art which would take considerable practice, Vivi and Marsh quickly realized. Even trying to play a simple, well-known song created problems of timing and harmonizing, but it was fun. Vivi kept dissolving into giggles to their sour notes.

"I give up, I give up," she gasped at length, pushing her folding chair away from the table. "Won't you play for us so we can hear how it really should sound?" she appealed to the instrument's maker, who was sitting back, enormously enjoying their efforts.

"We should have my wife here. Then we could play you some duets. She's the one who can really play and sing," he said regretfully, but he didn't hesitate to begin playing a single dulcimer.

The songs he sang were new to Vivi, and she had the feeling they were his own compositions. As he sang, he held her gaze, as if serenading her—or, in view of his mischievous glances at Marsh, serenading her on Marsh's behalf.

One was a lively, humorous ballad about excuses— the excuses people offered for not doing the things they should, particularly attending church. Ruefully, Vivi acknowledged the truth of those lyrics. Well, she had already determined to begin attending services regularly.

From that song, the old gentleman eased into a plaintive love melody.

> I never knew how sweet a kiss could be
> Till I met you.
>
> I never knew what love songs were about
> Till I met you.
>
> I never wanted to marry and settle down
> Till I met you.

Marsh's arm tightened about Vivi's waist as they

stood watching and listening. She glanced up at him, and her eyes widened at what she saw in his and at the realization of what she herself felt.

Love. Deep and warm, steadfast. It grew to fill her, reassuring and powerful.

And confusion swiftly followed it.

How could she be in love with Marsh Henderson when she already had Barry? She couldn't possibly be in love with two men at the same time. Attracted, perhaps, but in love? Hadn't she already decided she felt only friendship for Marsh? Well, yes, and physical attraction, too. But she'd assured herself that her love for Barry was powerful enough to conquer the passing fancy for another personable man.

Now she wasn't sure of anything, except that she'd never even imagined feeling what she felt for this man at her side. *Till I Met You.* Friendship. A deep matching of interests. And the desire to touch, to share, to respond to his every glance and caress.

How long did they stand gazing into each other's eyes? Vivi realized that the song had ended, that the elderly gentleman was merely plucking strings at melodic random. Some other people had drifted up to listen and watch and to ask questions.

"Shall we go?" Marsh softly suggested. "Do you want to look at anything else?"

Silently, Vivi shook her head. She walked outside as if in a daze.

When had their friendship turned to love? How could it? The questions kept spinning in her mind.

And Barry. When she was with him again, and Marsh wasn't around, then how would she feel? Barry had already been disappointed, by one woman. His failed marriage already made him shy away from commitment. Now if she compounded that hurt, the effect upon him could be disastrous and permanent.

In silence they got into the car, and she started the engine and began to drive, automatically following the Yellow Route markers south and east through the glowing wooded countryside. Neither she nor Marsh had anything to say. Odd, she reflected. She'd always imagined that the discovery she was loved by the man whom she loved would be an ecstatically happy moment. Now she was troubled. Almost in shock.

"Find a place where we can stop," Marsh directed. "We have to talk, Vivi. Your grandmother's house isn't the place."

Vivi nodded. Too many people were in and out of the house, not to mention Gran herself, sharp-eyed, knowledgeable. Privacy was what they needed.

Here was a small town. People in other cars had parked to walk around. Vivi eased into a parking slot, but neither she nor Marsh made any move to leave the car. They turned to survey one another, with worried eyes.

"This isn't how I thought it would happen, you know," he said quietly. "I always supposed that when I met *the* woman, she'd be someone I met at work or church, and love would come gradually. And we'd both be free. Instead, a week ago I came up those stairs to ask if you'd move your car, and you turned around and looked at me—and that was it." He spread his hands and shrugged. "Except the more I get to know you, the more it grows. That song said it all. Till I met you, I thought I'd been in love before, but now I know it wasn't even close."

Vivi's eyes, searching his face, were wide. "But I'm not free, Marsh. And we've only known each other a week. And I'm not a really strong Christian. That is, I was brought up to be, but I haven't been much of one for years. I'd like to begin again, but I've thought that before and haven't stuck to it."

He nodded, accepting her words. "I'm not asking you to commit yourself, Vivi. Either to me or to a church. It's meaningless if you're pressured into it. Just think about it. Maybe God's offering you a way back, some new choices. Take a long look at your job in St. Louis and at Barry. Keep in mind that I'm waiting. So is a job with my agency."

"Oh, Marsh—!" She gestured helplessly. "It's all so sudden, so—" She broke off, giving her head a little shake.

His hand covered hers, warm and reassuring. "I know. I said I'm not asking you to commit yourself. Not yet. Just to keep it in mind. Come visit Paducah. See the agency offices. Meet the rest of the staff. Then if you like what you see and things aren't working out in St. Louis, come to Paducah to live and work. There's no rush. We've got all the time in the world. I'm that sure of what we have between us."

Her smile was faint, quavery. This was too much too fast. It frightened her. How could she make such decisions when so much was at stake? If she chose him, she would hurt Barry who had already been hurt once. But everything about Marsh seemed so right. The confidence in his words warmed her spirit. She lifted her hand to touch his face lightly.

"We'd better get on back," she said softly and reached to turn the key in the ignition.

Move to Paducah. Work with him. Suppose she did quit and made the move, then didn't like it? Helping Marsh do those ads had been fun, but that was only one time. Perhaps she wouldn't like it as a regular job or wouldn't live up to his expectations. He'd said not everyone could do it. She'd have to return home, defeated, a failure.

Except she wouldn't fail. Somehow, Vivi felt an inner confidence of that. She was good at what she did, and she'd be even better at writing this kind of copy, particularly with Marsh's creativity energizing her. In any case, people in broadcasting constantly changed jobs and tried different cities. There was no stigma to quitting and returning.

Common sense dictated taking the most direct route back to town and to Gran's house. But Vivi hated to end this drive. It was the last one they'd take together. Only the weekend remained. Then the festival and their time together would be over. All weekend, the town and country roads would be so jam-packed with tourists that she wouldn't enjoy taking her car out.

"We haven't been to Billie Creek Village," she offered. "And I understand several buildings have been added to it since last time I was there."

"They add onto it all the time," Marsh concurred. "But I don't especially want to tackle it till I get off these crutches. And the Shades. I keep meaning to go up there and see why a state park would be named the Shades."

"Because it's shady?" Vivi hazarded. Here they were, talking of inconsequentials, like two chance-met strangers, when she would love to turn to him and take him into her arms. If she did, would she be seeking or offering comfort?

All too soon, they reached the Rockville square where all four sightseeing routes joined. Vivi was surprised to discover it was mid-afternoon. The day seemed to have flashed past. The more she wanted to prolong moments, the more speedily they passed.

"I suppose we should get back to the house," she said reluctantly. "There are some new guests arriving for the weekend. I need to help Gran welcome and settle them."

"I suppose," he echoed. "Vivi, I do love you. Keep that in mind, however this turns out. I don't want to add to your problems. Maybe I have, but not intentionally."

"I know. I appreciate that, Marsh. I just feel so—so confused. I have to have a breathing spell, to think it out."

At Gran's corner Vivi had to wait for the cross traffic to pass before she could make the turn. The big old white house rose ahead of them, hospitably waiting.

Several cars were in the broad driveway blocking Marsh's scarlet Corvette. One of them, although it looked vaguely familiar, was a new arrival. Vivi pulled in close behind a van and turned her head to smile at Marsh.

"Well…" he said, sounding as if he, too, hated to get out and go in. "What'll we do tonight?"

Vivi shook her head. "There's square dancing at the 4-H Building—"

He grinned. "Now, Vivi! Can you see me square-dancing on these crutches? Get serious, will you?"

She laughed, abruptly deciding not to ruin these last days—really hours—together by doubts and premature nostalgia.

"Then I suppose it's just a quiet evening talking or watching TV, if anything good happens to be on."

"Talking," he said reflectively. "We never seem to run short of things to talk about, do we?"

"Right. Well…" Reluctantly, she opened the door. "We had better go on in. Gran's probably wondering why we're just sitting here."

"Your Gran probably has a very good idea why we're just sitting here," he said sardonically. "Young at heart, that lady. If things do work out for us, won't she be happy?"

"Pleased as punch. I have an idea this's why she was so anxious to have me come visit and help again this fall."

Marsh grinned. "Most likely! I seem to remember, when I stopped by last summer to say hello and tell her I wanted to come stay during this festival, she showed family snapshots and mentioned her grand-daughter who was in advertising."

"That woman!" But Vivi was affectionate, not indignant. If only she hadn't already met Barry. If only…"Well… let's go on in. Need any help getting out?"

"For old times' sake," he said meekly. "If you please."

Smiling, Vivi went around the car and opened his door, to pull out his crutches from the back seat and then to give Marsh himself a hand in emerging. He teetered a bit as he got to his feet, and instinctively, Vivi grasped him, holding and steadying him.

Laughing, she looked up into his face. She knew from his expressions that under other circumstances he would have kissed her. As it was, his glance was a caress, speaking of his love and desire but his respect for her feelings prevailed.

The slam of the screen door and the sound of foot-steps crossing the porch made them turn, a greeting on the tip of their tongues.

As Vivi had expected, Gran was coming to join them. However, instead of her usual smile of welcome, Gran's brows were drawn together, and her mouth was a firm tight line.

Vivi's eyes widened in surprise, then spotted the man following Gran. The afternoon sun turned his fair hair to gold, and Vivi thought he looked familiar, somehow....

Then she took a second look, startled, as recognition dawned, impossible though it surely was.

Barry? Here? But this was Friday. He should be back in St. Louis, at work. Surely this was merely someone who bore a strong resemblance to him. Thinking of him so much made her see him in every fair man whom she encountered; this couldn't actually *be* Barry.

It was. And the car which looked familiar—it was Barry's car, which she knew as well as she did her own.

"Vivi," Gran said, sounding tart. "Your young man's here. He came just after lunch." She was disapproving. Because he'd been kept waiting all this time? But she had known Vivi and Marsh probably wouldn't be back before now.

Vivi looked beyond Gran to Barry himself, and received yet another surprise.

She'd assured herself—and Gran and Marsh—that Barry knew her and trusted her, that he wasn't the jealous type.

Ordinarily that might have been true. This afternoon, he fairly bristled as he stared challengingly at Marsh. His blue eyes were hard and suspicious, summing up a man he instantly recognized as a rival.

Marsh put his hand on Vivi's shoulder, as if needing

140

more support than his crutches offered. But he was claiming her. That was obvious to everyone present, and Vivi could feel his tension and hostility vibrating through the touch. Rivalry crackled in the air like heat lightning.

Vivi was literally in the middle. *And what*, she wondered a trifle desperately, *am I going to do now?*

Chapter Ten

"Look, sweets, I love you, and I want to be with you, but all this down-home business just isn't my style," Barry said, surveying the crowded square and grimacing as he stepped in a mud puddle left over from yesterday's rain. "Can't we go somewhere else?"

"I suppose...." Vivi consented, trying to think where, and fighting down disappointment. She had been so eager to share all this with him, to show him what she loved about the festival. "There's Billie Creek Village...." Unlike the theater and the scenic routes, it wouldn't be a constant reminder of Marsh.

"I was thinking more of going back to the real world," he said bluntly. He grinned teasingly. "You've been here so long, you've got hayseeds in your hair." He reached and tweaked a curly strand, pretending to pluck out some hay.

"This is pretty real," Vivi mildly protested with a smile. "Come on, Barry, you haven't given it a chance. People from all over the United States and Canada come to see this. The leaves and bridges are beautiful." Planning fast, she offered, "We could go on the Brown Route, we'd have time for that before getting back to

Gran's for supper, and then we could go to the theater. The play is hilarious."

"Supper?" he echoed with gentle mockery. "How about *dinner?* And if it's all the same to you, I've spent more than enough time with your grandmother for one day." He grimaced. "Do you have any idea how long I was there waiting for you? And what a cross-examination I got? All about my prospects and how come I'm divorced and whether I go to church and whether my intentions are honorable." He made a face. "I didn't tell her to mind her own business, but I felt like it. And how'd she get the idea that we're engaged?"

Vivi flushed a trifle. "Well, I'm afraid I told her that—but it was because she was starting to matchmake. She really likes Marsh Henderson."

"Well, I don't. He's a lot too interested in you."

Barry sounded possessive. Wasn't this exactly what she'd hoped would happen, that he'd realize how much she meant to him?

"I know. That's why I told them that we were engaged. And after all, we haven't been seeing anyone else."

"Yeah, well, it laid me open for a lot of questions about when we planned to tie the knot and whether it's going to be in a church and what church I go to." He sounded disgruntled, and Vivi couldn't blame him. Walking into that interrogation without any prior warning must have been unpleasant. "And she thought I should've bought you a diamond ring. Now, look, you know how I feel about marriage. I love you, but never again!"

"I know you had a bad experience," she soothed, "but not all marriages turn out bad. Anyway I don't

143

want to argue with you about that. I haven't been pressuring you about it, have I? Gran is really a fine person, and I think a lot of her. I'd like for the two of you to get along better, since you're both so important to me."

"Not tonight." He was immovable there. "Vivi, you know where I stand about the whole in-law bit. It's when they mix in that things start going wrong. Anyhow, I called in sick today and came all this way to spend time with you, not to walk around with a lot of other people or look at artsy-craftsy junk. As far as the leaves go, sure, they're pretty, but I saw enough of that on the trip over here. They can't hold a candle to you, anyhow. I want to be with you, look at you, not mess around with this stuff or sit talking to an old lady and her roomers."

"What do you want to do, then?" Vivi asked, irritated by his words and, more than that, by his tone and the way he looked at her. "Whatever you say."

"Whatever I say?" he teased. "Hey, sweets, you're asking for it, you know that?"

"Within reason," she smilingly amended. "The thing is, Barry, everything here is geared to the Covered Bridge Festival. I think there are pizza places and drive-ins along the highways, but that's about the size of it."

"I want something better than that for my *supper*." And he put teasing emphasis on the term. "Sweetheart, you have been out in the sticks so long, you're starting to talk like them. How do you stand it, a whole week? Bet you can hardly wait to get back to the real world, right? So, what d'you say to driving down to Terre Haute for a good meal and a movie or dancing or something? Maybe a movie *and* dancing. There's bound to be a place we can have a few drinks and dance a while, after the show."

"Dinner, at least," Vivi allowed. "Then we can see how we feel about doing anything more." Her expression was rueful, asking his understanding. "Not knowing you were coming, I put in a long, full day, and I have to be up early tomorrow morning to help Gran. I doubt if I'll be very interesting company after nine or ten o'clock."

"Nine or ten, the evening's just getting off to a good start then," he scoffed, but he gave her a hug. "Okay, okay. Dinner it is. What d'you say to steaks? Or sea food, maybe."

Up in her tower room, Vivi changed to her rose wool dress and applied makeup as swiftly as she could, uncomfortably aware of Barry downstairs with both Gran and Marsh. That was a touchy situation, and she wanted to rescue him from it as soon as possible.

Gran obviously disapproved of their going clear to Terre Haute for dinner. Face it, she disapproved of Vivi going anywhere with Barry, period. She just plain disapproved of Barry. Vivi doubted that Gran would approve of any man at all, now that her hopes had been raised where Marsh was concerned. She wanted him for a grandson, not some stranger.

And who knows what Barry might say or do, if provoked? Vivi couldn't blame him if Gran's attitude annoyed him into wanting to shock her. After all, he was the established man in Vivi's life, not the interloper. He could shock Gran without even trying, as far as that was concerned. His life was so much more sophisticated, he could unwittingly say something which would horrify an elderly lady who lived so quietly.

Moreover, Marsh was affable, yet there was a steely glint in those hazel eyes which spoke of his determination to fight for what he wanted. She didn't think he'd use unfair tactics, but he might encourage Barry to compound the bad impression he'd already made.

Definitely, she had to get Barry out of the house with all possible speed. Besides, she felt eager to spend time alone with him. Would her feeling for him revive then?

Wryly, as she combed her hair, Vivi conceded that he was not making a terribly good impression upon her, either, today.

Jealousy. Jealous behavior, as such was forgivable. And why did he have to keep talking about the real world? This seemed more real to her, the farming and traditional values, than the plastic people and settings of the city, at least the company which she and Barry kept there. They seemed to be seeking what people like Gran and Marsh and the old gentleman who made dulcimers already possessed.

When she came downstairs, Barry rose with alacrity. Gran's mouth was set in a prim line. Marsh glowered as he took in how she had fixed up; except for their evening at the theater, she'd worn jeans and casual tops, or at most a skirt, when going out with him.

Barry's humor improved as they left the house, then the town itself, behind. "This's what I like, having you all to myself," he said, smiling. "Hey, Vivi, what're you doing clear over there? Move closer, will you?"

"Keep your mind on driving and both hands on the wheel," she laughingly ordered. "There are some sharp curves on this road for a while." She couldn't snuggle up to him as she often did, not when she was unsure of her feelings.

"I'll be so glad to have you back at the station. It isn't the same without you," he declared, accepting her refusal with good grace. He took a bend fast enough to scare her, so perhaps that showed him what she meant. "*And*," he continued, "I've signed up some great new accounts, and I want you to write those spots. I've finally landed that car dealer I've been cultivating."

"Him?" The words popped out before Vivi could stop them. "Oh, Barry, I've heard so much about some of the unethical stunts he's pulled—"

"But nothing illegal. He wants to work on his image in these spots." He turned his head to grin at her. "Hey, sweets, he doesn't do anything all the other car dealers don't do. Grow up! And the place that puts on the rock concerts, we've snagged that account, too."

"Oh, I know that makes you happy." But she didn't feel easy about it. She remembered the quality of the previous ads for those concerts and the things she'd heard whispered about off-stage happenings there. Gran's questions returned to her, about writing ads for things she didn't believe in, and Marsh's comments, too, that she'd find writing copy at his agency far more to her taste.

She gasped as Barry's car slithered around another hilly turn. It came dangerously close to an oncoming car which had, admittedly, also swung wide. Barry's comments were colorful and violent. She began to be concerned about his driving when he brought her back to Gran's. It would be dark by then, and if he'd had the drink or two which he'd mentioned, which he usually did have when they went out....

Why was she so picky about him? He was just being himself. He always drove fast, but he had excellent reflexes. She couldn't fault him for being unhappy over the reception he received from both Gran and Marsh, even though she couldn't blame them, either. As for his swearing at that other driver, most people would. It was just that after this week among people who didn't swear, she noticed it.

She was being hypercritical. The attraction to Marsh now made her nit-pick where Barry was concerned. It was unfair of her. If she'd accepted these traits in the past, she had no right to criticize them now.

Barry went on to bring her up-to-date on station happenings, and Vivi relaxed, laughing appreciatively. He told a story well. She could see those incidents as he described them, and he expanded under her enjoyment, blue eyes agleam with laughter as he glanced at her in shared pleasure.

"Hey, how'd we get here already?" he interrupted himself to demand in surprise as they reached the stretch of freeway on the north edge of Terre Haute. "I swear it took me longer to drive, going the other way! We haven't even discussed where we want to eat."

"Don't look at me," Vivi said amiably. "I don't know the Terre Haute restaurants at all." Instantly she remembered the small Mexican place where she and Marsh had eaten.

"And I was counting on you to be the expert," he teased. "Well, the motel where I'm staying has a good restaurant. I ate there this noon, so I can vouch for it. If we eat there, I can sign for it and put it on my credit card along with the room."

"They usually do have good food," Vivi acknowledged. "I'm glad you thought to get a place to stay. There isn't any room to be had in the entire Rockville area. It's a long drive back and forth for you."

He shrugged that off, smiling. "You know I like to drive. And you're worth it. I've missed you so much all week. Have you missed me, too...just a little bit? Look," he conceded, "if you really want me to see that village place you were talking about and those bridges, then you've got it. Tomorrow, okay? It's your day. We'll do whatever you say. And I'll turn on the charm, win Grandma over.

"As for that hulk rooming there—forget it!" He grinned. "When Grandma said you had taken one of the guests for a ride to see the leaves and bridges and that he was lame, I pictured some senior citizen with gout! What happened to this dude? It's not the time of year for a ski accident!"

"The story is, he was felled by a hostile alien space-ship," Vivi said, exaggeratedly grave. At Barry's out-raged expression she clarified, "A little boy dropped a toy and Marsh stepped on it. If you really mean it about tomorrow, I know just the places to go. You'll enjoy it. Wait and see."

"I'll enjoy being with you," he said instead.

Vivi rode in silence, feeling guilty and confused. Barry loved her, and how had she repaid him? She'd fallen in love with Marsh. What kind of person was she? She felt a stranger to herself.

Barry drove through Terre Haute on Route 41, the very same route she and Marsh had driven earlier that week. Then Barry turned left into the parking lot of his large luxury motel, but instead of stopping up front near the restaurant, he circled around to the rear and parked by his room.

"I have to clean my shoes," he explained, when she gave him a questioning look. They were muddy from the afternoon walk, and he was fastidious as a cat about cleanliness and his appearance. "It'll only take a minute. Come on in with me and see my room."

Dubiously, Vivi followed as he unlocked the door and went inside.

It was a nice room, with a queen-size bed and big windows clear across the front. Barry's suitcase was on the rack by the dressing table, and he got a cleaning cloth and began restoring his tassel loafers to their normal gleaming shine.

"Here, look this over," he suggested, handing her the room service menu. "You know, we could stay right here and order in. Wouldn't that be fun?"

"Eating in the dining room, with other people around would be more fun," she said with smiling firmness. "I didn't get dressed up and come all this way to eat in here, my friend!"

"One of these days I'm going to catch you in a weak moment, and you'll give in," he predicted, grinning and undiscouraged. "And it will be more fun!" Both of them knew he didn't mean a room-service dinner.

"Finished?" she queried, looking at his shoes. "You can see your face in those; they can't possibly take a higher shine. And I want my supper. Dinner. Whatever."

"Whatever," he echoed, and followed her outside. "We can leave the car here and walk to the dining room. That's quicker and easier, and it'll give you a better look at the motel."

Vivi didn't mind walking, although it crossed her mind, as they strolled across the courtyard, that leaving the car there meant that they'd have to return to his room to get it. He might be more persistent then. He generally did apply all his powers of persuasion when he took her home at the end of their dates. She shrugged that off. She'd held her own then, and she would tonight, too.

The dinner menu was far more extensive than the room service card. Barry was never one to be the least bit stingy, and he urged her to have prime rib, teasing her because she wanted it medium-well rather than more rare. With the steak they ordered salad, baked potatoes with lavish sour cream, and pecan pie for dessert. He asked for a glass of ruby-red wine with his meal and ordered a glass of wine for her, as well.

"I don't know why you keep doing that. You should know by now that I won't drink it," she scolded. He invariably ended by drinking it himself.

"One of these days I'll catch you in a weak moment," he sing-songed in echo of his earlier remark. "Come on, loosen up. Enjoy. Get rid of these holier-than-thou hang-ups. Hey, your grandmother said you've been reading the Bible. She had to be kidding—wasn't she?"

"You know what a reader I am," she evaded, and immediately felt cowardly. "It's really very interesting, Barry. You should give it a try. You'd be surprised how many familiar quotes and stories there are in it. I'm really finding a lot of help there."

His glance was comically sceptical. "Oh, c'mon, now! You've got to be putting me on. You're talking to *me*, Vivi, not good old Grandma!"

"You keep telling me to try this and that, that I might like it. Maybe you should try this; *you* might like it," Vivi said, nettled. "There are new Bibles meant for people like us who are not Bible readers, and it *is* interesting and relevant. Otherwise why would people have read and reread it all these centuries?"

He shook his head, grinning. "Oh, sweetheart,

you've been brainwashed! We've got to get you out of there, give you emergency therapy. I wonder where the closest cult deprogrammer is?"

"Barry, will you please get serious for once?" Vivi protested. "You know that I—"

The arrival of their steaks and potatoes interrupted her. For the next few minutes, their conversation was minimal, limited to offering one another the salt and pepper and various toppings for the potatoes and commenting upon the size of the potatoes, the excellence of the steak.

Vivi was relieved to have it that way. She didn't want to get into an argument with him, especially about religion. Her own sentiments were too fragile to risk his scorn, his sophisticated quips. And hadn't she felt much the same, before actually starting to read? She'd picked up the Bible with a certainty that it would put her to sleep in a hurry.

Her mind kept straying from the elegant dining room to the other time she'd eaten in Terre Haute, that Mexican lunch. She wished she were back in that bright little fast-food establishment with Marsh. They'd been relaxed, joking and sharing their food. Now she was on guard, knowing that most of the subjects of greatest interest to her would bore or annoy Barry.

Her feeling for him wasn't reviving. Somehow, she had changed. Barry was just as he'd always been, a good-looking, charming, average young man, maybe no better, but certainly no worse, than most. The thing was, Marsh wasn't the least bit average. More than his height made him stand head and shoulders above most people.

Their dessert came, and Barry ordered Irish coffee,

again insisting upon getting one for her, too.

"Barry, I don't *want* any. You know I don't drink. Putting liquor in the coffee just ruins the coffee," she said, irritated by his persistence. "And I wish you wouldn't drink any more this evening, either. After all, you have to drive me home, and that road has some sharp curves and hills, remember?"

"I drive better after a few drinks than most people do cold sober," he claimed. "You'd do a lot better if you'd loosen up. Maybe then you wouldn't be so judgmental."

"I'm judgmental!" she echoed indignantly. "What have you been doing except passing judgment on me, my family, and everything I do and say—and everything you see—ever since you got here? Who appointed you judge and jury?"

He stared at her. "What's got into you?" he asked, genuinely surprised. "So don't I have a right to my opinion any more?"

"You certainly do. But so do I. That's what I don't like. You don't seem to want me to have any opinions which aren't carbon copies of yours."

"Oh, now, sweets, that isn't true," he protested. "I don't know how you can say that. I'm crazy about you. You just frustrate me, holding me at arms' length all the time. You're up-tight. Just try a sip of your coffee. See how good it tastes and how it relaxes you."

"Sure, it relaxes me right to sleep," Vivi said wryly. "A sleeping pill couldn't do it any faster." Perhaps the light approach and the thought of bringing the evening to a premature end would convince him.

Instead he grinned and offered, "Well, I've got a bed handy. I'd just tuck you in. C'mon, Vivi, what d'you say? We can take our drinks back to the room and watch some TV." His blue eyes were earnestly persuasive. "We'll be all alone—no interruptions...?"

Vivi stared at him in consternation. "Barry, you can't be serious." Except she knew he was. She had the strong suspicion that this was why he was staying here in Terre Haute, why he had suggested dining in Terre Haute, and at the motel restaurant—why he'd left the car at his room.

"I'm always serious where you're concerned," he assured her. "Sure. You've seen what a great room that is. Come on."

Firmly, she shook her head. "That's not for me, Barry, and you know it. We've been through all this so often in the past, I'm surprised you'd even bring it up."

His boyish charm thinned. "You're just playing hard to get. You want to be coaxed," he accused. "Otherwise you never would have come to my motel with me."

"That's not true, and you know it." She kept her voice low, but it quivered with indignation. "When you do the driving, you know you go precisely where you please."

They'd been through that in the past, too. She knew that he would have brought her here regardless of where she suggested dining, just as he'd driven around to park outside his room. He couldn't lay a guilt trip on her on that score. He had in the past, but not now.

"I didn't hear you making any protest," he charged, but at least he, too, spoke softly. "You're a tease, Vivi. You lead me on so you can slap me flat. And you're probably frigid, too."

"The way you're behaving doesn't tempt me to prove otherwise," she informed him. Repentance or indignation at his accusations were supposed to make her give in and "prove her love." In the past it had almost worked; only a timely interruption had given her a chance to think. Not tonight.

In chilly silence, they finished their pecan pie. Barry drank down his Irish coffee. Then with a defiant glance at her, he tossed down the contents of her untouched cup in a single gulp. He fumbled in his pocket for his billfold and slapped down an extravagant tip.

With dignity, Vivi proceeded him out of the restaurant, then turned to face him. "I'd like to go back to Rockville now, Barry."

"Why? The evening's young. Hardly started, in fact." He had a half-smile on his face.

"It's aged fast. Please take me home." She didn't particularly want to ride with him when he'd been drinking, but what choice did she have?

"Home? To St. Louis, you mean?" he teased, deliberately perverse.

"Home to where I'm staying now, home to my grandmother's house." By an effort, she hung onto her temper.

He considered. "No. I don't think I will," he said at length. "You aren't being very nice to me. Why should I be nice to you? Of course, maybe if you came back to the room with me and coaxed pretty-please… The car is over there anyhow…." His tone was tantalizing. "Know what I mean?"

Vivi knew exactly what he meant. But moral scruples aside, Vivi had never felt less like kissing anyone. She not only wasn't in love with him anymore, right now she didn't even like him.

"Barry, the evening is over. You've had too much to drink. Please take me home—or better yet, loan me your car and I'll drive myself, then bring it back tomorrow morning."

He leaned against the wall and crossed his legs in a negligent pose. "Nope. I don't feel like it. Come back to the room with me, and maybe I'll take you back to your good old Granny's. Maybe. About midnight. Or in the morning."

"Now," she emphasized, level-eyed. This couldn't be happening. "Barry, give me your keys."

"Nobody drives my car but me." He was smiling, enjoying having her in his power. "So what're you going to do about it, sweets?"

She hated that nickname. She never had really liked it, and now, he had spoken so sarcastically, she absolutely loathed it. She glanced around, hoping inspiration would come to her.

"I am going to go and sit down in the lobby," she informed him. That fell far short of inspiration, but it was the best she could do. "You have half an hour to come to your senses and quit playing silly games."

"Yeah? Then what're you gonna do? Walk?" Barry grinned, his glance sweeping down to her delicate high heels. "Well, I am going to my room. *You* come to *your* senses and quit playing silly games, huh? When you do, you know where to find me."

Vivi gave him an expressive look, her brown eyes sparkling angrily, then she pivoted and walked, stiff-backed with rage, over to the grouping of sofas and club chairs in the lobby, and sat down.

When she looked back at where he had been leaning against the wall, he was gone.

Now what was she going to do? Vivi opened her purse and took swift inventory of the cash in her billfold. She had no idea how much a taxi might charge

156

for a trip back to Rockville—even if she could find one that was willing to take her—but she knew it would be more than she had. Cabs didn't take credit cards, did they? And she'd left her traveler's checks back at Gran's.

She sat, feeling increasingly self-conscious, as if everyone who worked at the motel or passed through the lobby stared at her and talked about her. A few men did give her appraising looks, and she steeled herself in case one should come over and try to make a pick-up.

How could Barry put her in such a position? How *could* he? And she'd been worrying about hurting him by telling him her feelings had changed!

Time passed. Bitterly, she hoped Barry was enjoying his little game. He had to come to his senses, turn, apologize, and take her home soon…didn't he?

These thirty minutes were rapidly running out.

Vivi rose and wandered over to look at the magazines displayed for sale. Then she went into the ladies' room to comb her hair and re-do her lipstick.

"Oh God, what am I going to do now?" she said under her breath. The words on Gran's bookmark, "God is our refuge and our strength, a very present help in trouble," flashed through her mind. "God, I am in trouble, and I do need Your help," she said, glad that she was alone in the restroom. "What do I do now? What can I do?"

She stared at her reflection. And it came to her. This was a motel. They'd surely know whether there was a bus going to Rockville. And, if there wasn't any till morning, she had her credit cards and some cash. She could spend the night here. In a room of her own, *not* Barry's. It annoyed her to be put to that expense and inconvenience, but she could.

And there was a pay phone out in this short hallway between courtyard and lobby. She'd call Gran and tell her what had happened. A censored version. It was quite enough, to tell her that Barry'd been drinking and had become difficult and that she was reluctant to get in a car with him.

Vivi's upward glance encountered the exhaust fan, but her words were aimed higher. "Thanks. I feel lots better about everything now!"

The call to Gran was reassuring. "You stay right there!" Gran ordered. "I'll be right down to get you!" She snorted indignantly. "And even if that young man does come to his senses, don't you get in a car with him. Not if he's had too much to drink!"

Wandering back into the lobby, Vivi tried to figure how long it might take Gran to arrive. Gran would probably need to change clothes or at least shoes, maybe comb her hair, put on a coat, collect her purse, and tell somebody where she was going. And no doubt she would have to get cars moved so she could get her Buick out of the garage. She disliked driving after dark, so she would drive slowly. Ruefully, Vivi decided she'd better not hope for rescue to arrive in less than an hour. All due to Barry and his selfish, inconsiderate behavior!

It seemed hardly more than a half hour until she heard the guttural snarl of a sports car engine, the slam of its door—and then Marsh came striding through the entrance, to rake the lobby with a narrow-eyed, ferocious gaze.

"There you are," he gritted. "Where's that—that—"

"I don't know, and I don't care," Vivi declared with heartfelt relief. "Oh, Marsh—!"

158

He gathered her to him in a hard hug. "You *are* all right? He didn't hurt you—? If he did, I swear I'll— As it is, I'm not leaving here till he gets what he deserves!"

"Just take me home!" Vivi begged. "Marsh, please— don't cause a scene! He isn't worth it, and you—your ankle—"

For the first time, she realized he wasn't using his crutches. She drew back, staring up at his face, then down at his ankle.

Where were his crutches? And when he strode in through those doors and across to her, he hadn't had the slightest trace of a limp!

"Marsh Henderson, you can walk perfectly well!" she accused, brown eyes stormy. "And you drove your own car down here, didn't you? How long have you been lying to me? Was it fun, making a fool out of me? I'll bet you had a million laughs!" Her voice rose indignantly.

"Not in here," he muttered, as several heads turned to look their way. "Come on. Let's get started back. Your grandmother'll be worrying—"

"I don't know why she should," Vivi snapped hostilely, but she allowed him to hurry her on outdoors and to tuck her into the low-slung, luxurious sports car. "You've made such a wonderful recovery, and she thinks you're God's gift, anyway. Well, I don't! You're no better than Barry, when it comes down to the bottom line! Worse, maybe. Barry doesn't even pretend to be anything but what he is, while you—you—! Did you ever hear of 'Thou shalt not lie?' I expected better of a man who's supposed to be such a good Christian.

"You fooled me again, do you know that? I wondered whether you were a real Christian or just gave it lip service. Naive idiot that I am, you actually convinced me that you were for real!"

"Hey, now you wait just one minute!" Marsh protested, his deep drawl ominous. "You've got no right to accuse me of—"

The blast of a horn behind them made him realize that the Corvette blocked the motel drive. Angrily, he shifted gears, their clash betraying the turbulence of his feelings. The sports car shot forward with a jerk that threw Vivi back hard into her seat.

"Do please try not to kill us," she requested, freezingly polite. "I'd like to get back home tonight, alive and in one piece."

Chapter Eleven

"You trying to scrub the design clear off of that plate?" Gran inquired mildly.

Vivi looked down at the dish half-submerged in the sudsy hot water. She hadn't realized how long and vigorously she'd attacked its surface.

"I've heard of trying to wash a man right out of your hair, but not off a moss-rose breakfast plate," Gran continued. Her eyes were sharp and twinkled. "Is that what you're up to?"

"Is it obvious?" Vivi asked wryly. "Men! Right now I'm not crazy about any of them. They all take too much for granted. *And* they're all full of tricks."

"That so? I thought maybe you'd be pleased to see Marsh last night." Both tone and glance struck Vivi as overly innocent.

Vivi's stare raked her grandmother with suspicion. "And just how long have you known he could walk and drive that car of his perfectly well?"

"Well, maybe he did give his ankle just a little extra time to heal," Gran cautiously admitted. "And it may be, too, that hearing the predicament you were in made him forget about it."

Vivi snorted. "A likely story. Forget he was pretending, you mean! He just liked to be fussed over and waited on!" But, uneasily, she remembered he *had* been knocked unconscious. The doctor *had* instructed him to take it easy. He *had* shown his pain, that afternoon, and the next day, and even the day after that—Tuesday—when he accidentally put extra weight upon it.

"Most people do, when they're feeling poorly—and he was," Gran pointed out. "I know for a fact how upset he was. He didn't like you going out with Barry at all, and then when you called—my!"

"He was somewhat upset," Vivi conceded. "In fact, he was all for hunting Barry up. I'm not sure what Marsh intended to do to Barry, but I didn't want to be witness to it."

"Marsh did hit the ceiling," Gran agreed. "Reminded me of once when I went on a Sunday afternoon drive with a young fellow, and I ended up getting out and walking. Of course, we didn't go clear down to Terre Haute, and I had on better shoes for walking. I wasn't sure of your grandpa's feelings up till then. Of course, he wasn't your grandpa yet. We weren't even keeping steady company." Her smile was reminiscent, a little mischievous. "I don't mind a little righteous anger in a man."

Vivi didn't, either, she realized. "All the same," she complained, "*I* wasn't the one who had too much to drink. I didn't drink anything alcoholic at all, just iced tea. And I didn't stay with Barry at that motel. I didn't even know we were going to eat there. Marsh didn't need to take it out on me!"

"It happens, though. Like crying over a lost child, then warming its bottom when you find it. What'd

162

you say to him about being able to walk and drive his car?"

"Well—" Vivi was a trifle shamefaced. "The Bible may be full of miracles, but somehow I didn't much believe that was the explanation for his walking perfectly well or getting to Terre Haute as fast as all that." She looked around the kitchen. "I think that must be all the dishes. I'd better get to the beds."

Briskly she emptied the dishpan and rinse water, then headed for the stairs. This morning she felt the need for activity. Stripping sheets off beds and whacking pillows to fluff them provided good emotional therapy. There weren't many beds to do today. Most of last night's guests would stay tonight, as well.

Marsh had left the house directly after breakfast. Was he still furious at her, or was he prudently avoiding her until her own temper cooled?

Uneasily, she remembered. Those were extremely harsh accusations she'd flung at him. She'd called him a liar and a hypocrite.

But...was he? His reaction had been utter outrage, indignant denial.

Of course. Wouldn't he deny it just as much if it were the truth as if her charges were unjust?

Vivi could think of other motivations which were just as distasteful. Marsh couldn't be one of those men—could he?—who were ardent only as long as the woman in question was inaccessible, but then shied away once she freed herself of other ties?

An article she had read in one of Gran's magazines came to mind. It had discussed the problems which could arise in marriage if one partner was deeply devout and the other one lukewarm or completely uninterested in religion.

Anyway if Marsh's faith was sincere, could her own lack of Christian commitment have caused him to have second thoughts? But he'd known that ever since they'd discussed it last Sunday afternoon, and it hadn't noticeably discouraged him. She had even mentioned it when they parked to talk yesterday, and he'd seemed to take it in stride.

Or could it be because she'd gone out with Barry at all, yesterday afternoon and evening? But Marsh knew that she had to see Barry, break off with him, before she'd be free.

Could Marsh have cleared out today, because he didn't trust himself in case Barry appeared at the door to make up with her?

She *had* mentioned their touring plans to Marsh last night on that nightmarish drive home. She'd declared that Barry needn't show up today expecting everything to be the same between them.

As Vivi punched a pillow and thumped it down on the bed she determinedly dismissed all such speculation from her mind. There wasn't the slightest use going over and over this. She just had to wait till she could ask Marsh straight out.

Vivi stayed alert for the sound of either the telephone or a car stopping outside. She didn't actually expect Barry to come spend the day sightseeing with her, for all that they'd planned to. However, he was quite capable of waking this morning, repentant, and coming as if nothing had ever happened yesterday at Terre Haute. Or calling to see whether she was still too angry for it to be worth his while to go ahead and drive up here.

Well, this time all his charm wouldn't restore her good humor. He'd humiliated her and upset Gran and touched off that quarrel with Marsh.

All the cars turning onto this street cruised straight on past, just tourists in search of parking. The phone remained silent.

Gran began vacuuming the upstairs carpets. Vivi finished the beds, bundled up the sheets and pillowcases from the beds she'd changed, and took them downstairs. In the front hall, she dumped them down onto the floor by the telephone, hunted up the motel number, and placed a call to Barry there. She'd say she was from the television station, in St. Louis.

However, when the motel desk clerk consulted the room number, she told Vivi, "I'm sorry, he has already checked out."

"Oh, I thought I might still be in time to catch him," Vivi said, as calmly as though this were only the business call she was pretending. "Could you tell me what time he left?"

"Let me see... just before eight o'clock. Eight this morning," the clerk said.

"Oh," Vivi said. The time which Barry had checked out told Vivi a great deal, a great deal indeed. It was almost three hours ago. He ordinarily slept late on weekends. He must have had a sleepless night. He hadn't come back here, so the chances were that he actually was on his way west, returning to St. Louis. "Thank you very much."

Vivi stood staring at the phone a minute longer. She'd pretended that she was calling from St. Louis, that she was at the TV station now. A white lie. But how different was that from Marsh's pretense that he still needed his crutches, that he still couldn't drive his car? And he *had* said, the day of their picnic, that his ankle was better. Did she have any right to be so outraged?

And what if Marsh thought that she was the rejected one, that Barry had dumped her? Would he think she was only turning to him now because she no longer had Barry?

I've got to think of something else. Anything else!

Vivi carried the sheets and pillowcases down to the laundry room in the basement and started the first load on the wash cycle. Then she turned and began the long climb back up to her own room.

When she reached the tower, she eyed the Bible. Reading it last night had soothed her and made sleep possible. She was tempted to open it now, but Vivi knew that if she did, she wouldn't close it soon, and she had things to do.

For a moment she stood at the window, gazing out at the big old trees and the street below. So much had happened since her arrival, since the Friday afternoon when she'd stood here and Marsh had startled her by his silent approach. Then she had thought she was in love with Barry. Now...

How could her sentiments undergo such drastic reversal? She seemed to be a stranger to herself.

Vivi turned and rummaged in her purse to find that letter of Barry's in the zipped pocket. She had carried it there as the safest place. She didn't want Gran to find it accidentally and read it.

Now, rereading it without fantasy tinting her view, Vivi found it distasteful. The careless misspellings, the talk of the party, drinking and hangovers and living together. So many of the things which he said and did now seemed repugnant. This week away had stripped the blinders from her eyes.

"You know, Kitticat, I really dread going back to St. Louis and my job?" she confided to the little cat, which had followed her up to the tower room and sat on the bed, blinking at her with wide, intense golden eyes. "Oh, well, I like St. Louis. And I like the station and copywriting. It's just that I'm out of place in that crowd."

At this time day after tomorrow, however, she would be back at her desk. She had no other choice. Even quitting wouldn't eliminate that necessity, for she had a moral obligation to give work notice. Often the person who was leaving was even asked to stay on a little longer than the usual two weeks, till someone could be hired and trained.

How was Barry going to act on Monday morning when they both came in to work? And how would she act?

"Breaking up with him and avoiding him would at least help me avoid most of the others," Vivi thought aloud, sitting down on the edge of the bed to pull Kitticat onto her lap and rub around her chin and ears.

But she and Barry were in close contact over the advertising campaigns.

"I wonder if I would like working at a Christian station?" she said thoughtfully.

Were there any in St. Louis? If Terre Haute had one, surely a city the size of St. Louis would have one, maybe even several.

She wasn't a Christian, not what they'd consider a Christian. Did they hire people who weren't?

"Maybe if I talked with them, explained—?" she murmured tentatively. If they were truly Christians, wouldn't they understand that she was seeking a better way of life and extend a helping hand?

167

And there was the problem of making ends meet. Somehow, Vivi had a feeling they might not pay as well as other stations, particularly to start. She couldn't live much more economically than she now did, so she couldn't afford to change to a job which offered less money.

Marsh's agency was in Paducah. He'd offered her a job. He'd said the cost of living there was lower than in St. Louis.

Had he been serious? He had repeated the suggestion. He'd urged her to come and at least see the agency and Paducah. He'd mentioned a possible salary. That sounded serious.

Except she'd kept telling him no, no, it was out of the question. Probably by now their new copywriter had already been hired. They wouldn't create a job just for her.

Anyway, that was then. Now Marsh wasn't acting the same. If he wasn't avoiding her today, he was giving a good imitation of it.

"Well, I'm not going to sit around here moping, Kitticat," Vivi declared. She gave the cat a pat and put her back onto the bed, and stood up. "I'm going to shower and change and go buy souvenirs on the square." She grinned. "And who knows, maybe I'll even run into Marsh over there? I did a week ago, and I wasn't even trying, then!"

Rockville was bustling. Fine Indian summer weather and the last weekend of the Covered Bridge Festival combined to generate a turnout. By the time Vivi reached the square itself, the sidewalks were crowded, and she was forced to slow to a snail's pace.

Long lines waited to buy ham-and-bean dinners.

People waited, too, in front of the other serving huts, to buy chicken-and-noodle plates—baked potatoes slathered with sour cream, chives, and bacon-bits—ham or sausage sandwiches—hot sugared crullers—ice cream.

Underfoot, the grass which had been so thick and green a week ago was worn flat, brown, and thin. In a few days the lawn would be reseeded, and next spring it would be as lush as ever.

Will I revive as well as that grass? Vivi felt almost afraid to hope.

If only she'd see Marsh! A week ago when she'd come here, she had run into him at every turn and couldn't get rid of him. Now when she would welcome the sight of him, she couldn't spot his tall form anywhere. However, as on that other Saturday, her small stature made it difficult for her to see far in this sea of larger people.

Vivi had a short shopping list to fill. A few people back home merited souvenir gifts. Her parents, Jill, herself. Strike Barry off the list.

In addition to homemade egg noodles, cookies, a coffee cake, jams, and candy, Vivi bought notepaper which depicted various Parke County covered bridges. And she selected gourds and bunches of bittersweet and Indian corn to combine in seasonal centerpieces.

Bittersweet. What an appropriate thing to buy on a day like today. The brilliant orange of its berries contrasted with its name just as her own hopes and fears warred with one another. Had she found the man whom she truly loved, only to inadvertently ruin everything between them?

Although she didn't see Marsh himself, Vivi encouncountered some reminder of him everywhere she turned. The hoop-skirted doll lamp she'd teasingly assured him was precisely what he needed. The green calico snake with which he'd threatened her.

And when she wandered inside the courthouse, there were the paintings they'd looked at together. Now she smiled with painful affection at the one with the odd-looking sheep. Some of the others which she remembered liking were gone now; she imagined they sold well as festival souvenirs.

A small oil painting caught her eye. That had to be the Narrows Bridge. Yes, for there were the rocky outcroppings along the bank, where she and Marsh had picnicked. The painting was beautiful, and Vivi's first impulse was to buy it.

No. She didn't want a reminder of today, and if she couldn't clear up whatever had gone amiss between her and Marsh, she didn't want a memento of that golden day when they'd picnicked and shared a first kiss at the bridge.

When she went back outdoors, the food lines had dwindled. With scant enthusiasm, Vivi got a sausage sandwich and cup of coffee and wandered on across the courthouse lawn as she ate. At another booth she got an ear of buttery corn on the cob, then finished with a cinnamon delight for dessert. They left her feeling a little too full and no more cheerful.

Vivi glanced at her digital watch, debating what to do next. She'd seen everything here and was tired of being jostled in the crowd. She might as well go back to Gran's. The new guests were likely to start arriving any time now, and Gran really shouldn't have to run up and down the stairs all afternoon.

Besides, Marsh might be back, waiting for her.

And if Marsh weren't there, she'd settle down either on the porch or in the living room and wait till he returned.

Vivi had a long wait, although she couldn't settle anywhere. The new guests arrived, and they were a lively and talkative couple, making frequent calls upon her for information. They were curious about the big old house, wanting to know all about its history and its furnishings. They told about various other interesting places they'd visited and items which they themselves had collected.

They'd been in and around Rockville all day, on the square and out driving the Red Route and Yellow Route. Companionably they showed off what they had purchased and the Polaroid snapshots they had taken.

"And oh, those scarecrows!" the wife exclaimed reminiscently. "I love all the scarecrows anyway, but those men out on the Yellow Route who dressed up like scarecrows—did you see them?" And when Vivi said she hadn't, the woman went on, "Oh, you've got to go! They sit as still as…as…well, as scarecrows! Then after somebody's posed for a picture with them, they come to life! Oh, it's hilarious!"

When the new couple bustled back up to their room to prepare to go out to dinner, Vivi slipped away, too, heading up the back staircase to her tower room. She couldn't stay downstairs alone with Gran. Gran didn't ask questions or say anything, but obviously she knew and understood.

"I might as well get packed," Vivi muttered under her breath, looking around the circular room once she reached it.

Really, only this evening and tomorrow morning remained. And in the morning she would be doing all the usual morning chores, one last time.

A good share of the morning would be filled with going to church. Vivi looked forward to the services. Funny how a week had changed her attitude.

So this evening was really the logical time for her to pack her possessions in her plastic shopping bags. Then if her situation was no better tomorrow than it was today, she would head back to St. Louis.

She'd intended to stay until Monday afternoon, to help Gran do the final laundry and put the house back to rights after all the hubbub of festival guests. Hardly any of the people would stay here for Sunday night, however, and most of the finishing-up chores could be done tomorrow after church.

Vivi hated to strip her tower room of her belongings. She didn't want to leave. With tears springing to her eyes and blurring her vision, Vivi pulled garments from the armoire shelves and hangers, folded them, and slid them into the bags. Jeans, T-shirts, woven tops, underwear. She left out only the dress she'd wear to church tomorrow, the shirt and clean jeans she'd wear to drive home, and the batiste gown she would wear tonight.

A few things remained out on the nightstand and the bureau top. She could scoop her little travel clock and toiletries into a bag at the last moment. In the meantime, they helped sustain the illusion that she was still staying here.

"I wonder whether Marsh's packed any of his things yet?" she murmured to herself. Then her breath caught in an audible gasp.

What if he'd completely packed—and left?

Gran hadn't told her that he had. Surely Gran would

172

have. And he hadn't left this morning.

No, but Vivi herself had been out of the house all that time, over at the square. He could have returned then, packed, and departed. Since getting back to the house, she hadn't actually had time alone with Gran to talk. Too many other people had been around.

Only the soft soles of her shoes kept Vivi from clattering as she raced down the stairs. She had to find out. Would she find his room stripped and bare or find Gran's belongings replaced on the dresser and bureau top?

Only as she threw open the closed door of his room did it occur to her that he might have returned and that she would find him in there—even undressed. How embarrassing—

He wasn't. The room was empty of life. However, there were his brushes and his aftershave on the dresser.

Vivi stepped inside, feeling the need to be close to his possessions if she couldn't be close to the man himself. Her fingers touched his brush in light caress. She pulled out a gleaming dark hair entwined amid the bristles to twist it about her finger like a ring.

Something was missing. His attaché case wasn't in its usual place between bed and chair.

His Bible was open on the bedside table, however. It was a small leather-bound Bible, not the large one full of footnotes and cross-references which he had mentioned to her on several occasions.

Had Marsh, too, turned to the Bible's verses for comfort last night after their angry exchange?

Vivi stepped over and bent to look, curious to see which verses he had been reading.

She recognized it immediately—the Song of Songs, The Song of Solomon:

> While I slept, my heart was awake.
> I dreamed my lover knocked at the door.
> Let me come in, my darling,
> My sweetheart, my dove.

The guttural snarl of a sports car motor, its headlights sweeping the side of the house, made Vivi straighten guiltily.

Hastily, she slipped out of his room. He mustn't find her in there, prowling among his belongings. It'd be bad enough if he entered the house to find her in the living room, as if she were waiting for him.

Of course, she was waiting for him. She was anxious to see him, to apologize, to straighten out whatever had kept them apart all of today. But, simultaneously, she was afraid. She wasn't sure she wanted to see him yet, not till she knew what she was going to say to him.

Then, as she hurried into the kitchen and started back upstairs, a sense of wonder began to fill her.

There was still hope. There had to be. Otherwise, would Marsh have been reading the timeless beauty of the lyrical love poetry?

"Think positive," Vivi said under her breath, her eyes aglow. "Last night I slept, too, but my heart was awake. I wonder how I'll sleep tonight?"

Chapter Twelve

"Of all the times to be chaperoned!" Vivi later complained to Kitticat, as the little cat watched her get ready for bed. "Where were those people when I *wanted* to have somebody around?"

The evening would have been pleasant—if she had not hoped for time alone with Marsh. Except for a few guests who went to the play at the Ritz, everyone stayed in, drawn by the lively new couple.

As if they were at a family reunion, people laughed and talked, exchanging tales of their hobbies and jobs and comparing notes about the Covered Bridge Festival. They talked about what they'd found to eat, souvenirs they'd bought, pictures they'd taken.

Marsh certainly seemed to enjoy it. He ignored a perfect opportunity to be alone with her when she went out to the kitchen to fix a snack tray, a platter of Gran's cookies and glasses of cider for everyone.

Ordinarily he would have followed her to talk, to tease. This evening he was deep in conversation with one of the men, and he didn't even seem to notice that she'd left the room.

Maybe he'd lost interest in her. Maybe—maybe—.

was so frustrating not to be able to catch his eye, to manage a few minutes alone to find out! She'd assumed he'd take the initiative, as he had before. He didn't.

So she had to. She didn't intend to leave Rockville or allow Marsh to leave before they straightened out whatever had gone wrong between them. She didn't know how or where to begin, but she was determined to do it.

Barry's letter was still hidden away in the zipped inner compartment of her purse. Vivi didn't quite know what to do with it. She didn't really want it, yet it was worth keeping in case she began to weaken and needed to remind herself what she found distasteful about Barry.

She was finished with Barry. And he was not an influence, of any sort, on her. Marsh had to believe that.

Strange. She'd thought Marsh had come into her life to test her love for Barry, that if she was able to withstand a man as attractive as Marsh, it would prove she could withstand anything.

In actuality, it was just the opposite. Barry was the test, the temptation. He was handsome and persuasive, hard to withstand, talking of love and exerting pressure upon her to abandon the moral standards which had always been so important to her.

And because she was a warm and loving person, wanting a home, a husband, and children, she'd been susceptible to a personable charmer.

She'd seen in Barry virtues which didn't truly exist. She'd felt he needed only time and love to recover from the trauma of a bad marriage and disagreeable separation and divorce. Now, for the first time, Vivi wondered what the real cause of that divorce had been. She'd heard his version, but what would his former wife tell?

Oh, Barry wasn't a villain. Probably neither of them had been wholly to blame or wholly innocent. He was simply an average young man who had grown up without any religious training, a typical representative of the "Me-First" generation. His motto was "If it feels good, do it," without considering that behavior from a moral standpoint. The Ten Commandments, the laws of conduct which had been so workable for thousands and thousands of years, were called square by Barry and his friends.

To a person like that, marriage—even if he had ever become willing to marry again—was nothing to build upon. It was like building a house on shifting sands. How very fortunate she'd been that Barry hadn't wanted to get married. Coming to spend these days with Gran had turned out to be precisely what she needed to see how she was drifting into danger.

True, she'd worriedly recognized that their different viewpoints would cause problems. She'd merely felt determined to solve those problems. Her love, she was certain, could change Barry, could restore his faith so they could make mutual commitments, both emotionally and legally.

In the long run, she was the better for this experience. She'd emerge stronger for it—like flame tempered steel.

Gran and Marsh had been right. Not just when each had said Barry didn't really love her or he'd give her a ring. But also when they said that she wouldn't take a vacation away from Barry if she loved him as deeply as she'd thought. Infatuation was close to love, but it had the brief hot brilliance of a camera flash, not the long-lasting warmth of a well-banked fire.

Easing into bed, Vivi picked up the Bible from the nightstand, but instead of turning to the place which the bookmark held, she went back to The Song Of Solomon, the Song Of Songs.

Was this indeed an allegory of God's love for His chosen people or Christ's love for the church, as the introduction said? Vivi found it hard to believe anyone in love could read it as other than one lover's praise of a sweetheart.

"Like an apple tree among the trees of the forest, so is my dearest compared to other men. I love to sit in its shadow...."

Yet if one human could love another so deeply, how much greater would the supernatural love of the Almighty be? She read on, seeking to understand, wishing that she could ask Marsh about some of these things or read the annotated Bible of which he'd spoken. She was becoming aware of how ignorant she was, stumbling in the dark with a candle flame, the faintest of guides.

Tonight, when Vivi switched off the bedside lamp, her prayers were consciously directed to the Almighty, not merely *Oh, I hope* or *I wish that,* nor desperate like the plea which she'd murmured in the motel restroom *Oh, God, what do I do now?*

With concentration, she gave thanks for particular blessings which she had been granted, and then she made earnest supplication to be shown what she should do to become the person she wanted to be and how to go about doing it. She realized that it wouldn't be easy, that she'd undoubtedly encounter temptation and discouragement.

Vivi fell asleep before she finished. The sleep was

restless. Several times she woke to drift, not quite asleep yet not fully awake either, and she made other attempts to complete what she wanted to say, before sleep claimed her once more.

She felt positive that she was awake, wide awake, the last time. She could see the luminous dial of the little clock on the nightstand and the shifting patterns created by the moonlight shining through the branches of the old maple tree.

This time, instead of starting from the very beginning again, she merely lay praying wordlessly for help, for guidance—to know what she should do and to have the strength of character to do it.

And then, although the tower room's physical temperature and light remained unchanged, it seemed to fill with a warmth, and Vivi was surrounded by a powerful sensation of comfort, of knowledge, and of reassurance.

She felt loved, embraced, and encouraged. The help she prayed for, she would receive. She would be aided, directed, in the path she should take.

The travel alarm beeped electronically, and Vivi opened her eyes to early morning light. Six-thirty. She had time to ease awake before she had to jump out of bed and hurry to bathe and dress to help start breakfast.

Last night…had that assurance really happened? Things of that sort simply didn't happen to an ordinary, down-to-earth person like her. Anyhow, it had to be a dream. Some dreams were unbelievably realistic and vivid.

Except—she held a deep inner conviction that she had actually experienced it. She'd wakened knowing exactly what she should do, what she wanted to do.

Dream or no dream, it felt real, and she felt more positive than she had ever felt before.

She wanted to do more than live *like* a Christian, she wanted to *be* a Christian. She wanted to use her writing ability for something better than rock concerts and used-car dealers who wanted to improve their images while conducting shady business deals. And she wanted to marry a man she could admire and respect as well as love.

She'd kept protesting that her home, her job, all of her family and friends, were in St. Louis. However, the Bible was full of stories of people leaving all that was familiar and dear to them. Abraham, Moses, and perhaps the most famous—Ruth and Naomi, which she had reread just the other night.

"Who knows—maybe I'll be an even better Christian for having been around Barry and that crowd," Vivi murmured under her breath. "I certainly appreciate people like Gran and Marsh more now. Now I know the difference, just how fine Gran and Marsh really are."

Showering and dressing a little later, she wondered. All her life she had heard of born-again Christians, without knowing precisely what that term meant. Now she felt as if *she* had experienced some sort of rebirth.

Vivi reached the kitchen ahead of Gran, to set the juice glasses on a tray, the bread near the toaster, the eggs handy to the range. Quietly she began arranging the plates and silverware on the dining room table. She boiled water and poured it into the coffee pot to begin brewing.

She herself ate a much lighter breakfast than they served the guests. A slice of whole-wheat toast, spread with Gran's own blackberry preserves, and a glass of tomato juice satisfied her. She'd sat looking out the bay window, waiting for the coffee to finish brewing. "Can you spare an advance snack for a hungry man?" Marsh's voice came from the doorway into the dining room. His eyes lingered on her as if hungry for more than food.

"Of course." She rose quickly, wary yet hopeful. She nodded him to a seat across the table from her and went to check the coffee's progress. When she returned with his coffee, her resolve was firmer. "Marsh—I'd really like to talk to you—" Her brown eyes appealed to him for help. If only he'd meet her half-way...

"Talk away," he invited. "No time like the pres—"

"Mercy sakes, why didn't anybody wake me up?" Gran demanded, hurrying into the kitchen. "I've got to go buy myself a new alarm clock. That one I've got can't be depended upon at all! Although," she added thoughtfully, as she began breaking eggs into a big bowl and whisk-beating them into a golden froth, "once the festival's over, it won't make any difference what time I wake up. Not till this time next year. *Maybe* at the Maple Sugar Fair, come February-March."

"Now I know what I can give you for Christmas," Vivi quipped, giving Marsh a comically rueful look. No time like the present? The present was no time to talk, either.

His smile at her was as warm as if yesterday and the evening before had never happened.

"Maybe we could leave for church a little early?" he suggested. "Or go for a walk afterward? For now, I'll take these and get out of your way." He took his plate and coffee cup and eased out of the kitchen.

"A little early," Vivi called after him, and added to herself, "And maybe that walk afterward, too."

"My, my, sounds like things are improving between you two," Gran commented. "The atmosphere in this kitchen has lightened up, that's for sure."

"We're working on it," Vivi assured her.

"Maybe I came in at the wrong time?" Gran suggested, cocking her head questioningly.

Vivi shook her head. "Probably the right time, since we've got a houseful of people who'll be coming down to eat breakfast any minute now."

And now she had more incentive than ever to be efficient in the cooking and cleanup. Marsh had said a little early—how early was that?

As early as she could make it, she made up her mind. She'd get ready, and then wait, if necessary.

This rose wool-jersey dress was getting a work-out, Vivi reflected, as she changed later. And to think, she'd wondered whether she'd wear it, when she packed it to bring. Church twice, the theater, and dinner with Barry down in Terre Haute. Well, three out of four wasn't bad.

She smiled, feeling almost benevolent about Barry. What a favor he'd inadvertently done her, in showing off to such bad advantage.

Marsh was waiting in the living room when she descended the handsome old staircase. Her step hesitated as she looked at him sitting, not yet aware of her, reading the fat Sunday newspaper. He was clean-shaven, his hair was freshly combed, and his deep-brown suit was so beautifully tailored. Gold gleamed at his cuffs and on his Italian silk tie. He was a wonderful man, both in looks and in character. Could she ever begin to match him?

Then Marsh felt her gaze on him, and he glanced up, to smile and rise with swift anticipation when he saw her, and he strode across to join her at the foot of the stairs.

"It's so nice to see you *not* limping," she said impulsively. He moved beautifully, with such strong, wholly masculine grace.

"Crutches did sort of get in the way," he allowed. "You ready to start?"

She nodded. Gran knew why they wouldn't be walking with the rest of the group. Going across the porch and down the front steps, Vivi glanced up at him mischievously.

"Well…" he said, grinning sheepishly. He reached for her hand as they turned onto the sidewalk. Interlacing fingers, they swung hands as they strolled along together. "Vivi—I said things I didn't mean, and I'm sorry. I was upset, but that's no excuse."

"*You* were upset?" she questioned ruefully. "You weren't the only one, were you? I said quite a few things I've regretted, too. I wanted to tell you yesterday. I—I missed you."

"Oh, darling, not half as much as I missed you!" he groaned eloquently. "But I knew Barry had planned to come back up here to spend the day with you—"

"He had, but after Friday evening, did you really think he would? Or that I'd let him stay, if he did have the nerve to show up? No way!" she declared indignantly.

"I figured he'd come to his senses, realize what he'd lost in you, and come up here to apologize. The man's got to be the world's biggest nerd, to have you for his girl and let you get away!"

Vivi chuckled, warmed by the outspoken sentiment and amused at the thought of Barry, who considered himself the most with-it of men, being called a nerd. "He didn't. So?"

Marsh shrugged broad shoulders. "So while the two of you were out walking around the square Friday afternoon, I got on the phone and lined up a business call or two for Saturday, so I could keep busy and not have to see the two of you together." His glance at her was hesitant. "Then I wanted to ask you to go along with me. Only yesterday morning—"

Vivi winced expressively. Only too well did she remember yesterday morning. It hadn't been all Marsh. She'd given him the cold, silent treatment.

"So, at least we've got today. We can make the most of it. And I'll manage to get to St. Louis, just as soon as I can." His glance had a threatening scowl. "And if I get there and find you've made up with that—"

"You don't need to worry about that," she cut in, definite and convincing. "Marsh—when I go back in to work Tuesday morning, I'm going to turn in my resignation. Not just because of Barry, although he's a part of it. I want to get clear away from that whole crowd. You were right. That atmosphere isn't congenial for me."

He stopped dead, turning to her and reaching to take her other hand as well, his eyes scanning her face, hope dawning on his. "Then—are you going to come to Paducah?"

"Do you still want me to?" she countered, and she held her breath waiting for his answer.

"*Want* you! Vivi, there's nothing in God's green

184

world I want more! Look—I know you need time to find yourself. I am not asking you to leap into anything." His voice was deep and convincing, his hazel eyes were intent. "Come visit the company. If you come on a weekday, you can meet the rest of the staff and see the town. And if you like all you see, the job's yours. So am I. But there's no rush there, either. I'm so sure of what we've got, we can take our time building it. This isn't like a now-or-never infatuation. It's going to last. You will come?"

"I will," Vivi said, making a vow—a marriage vow. Her fingers returned the firm pressure on his, and her face was lifted to return his direct gaze as she gave him his answer. "I'm not sure when, but as soon as I possibly can. Oh, and Marsh—last night the strangest thing happened; I might have been dreaming it, but—" Swiftly she described the sensation of protective warmth, of reassurance, which had enfolded her. "I'm sure now. I want to lead a better life. And I'll need help. Preferably yours," she added with a twinkle.

"You've got it," he said fervently. "Have I ever been praying to hear you say that! Oh, Vivi!"

They strolled on, reaching the square, and wandering around it, feeling as if they were in a blissful world of their own. They were hardly conscious of all the other people who shared those streets with them. Most were tourists, but at this hour many were fellow worshipers, headed for the red-brick church at the southwest corner of the square, or the contemporary church a short distance to the east.

"You're going to wear my ring," Marsh declared, halting to look at the jewelry shop's show window as they reached it. "This all started in Rockville, so we're going to get our rings here. And it'll be a double ring ceremony, with a ring for each of us. *And* an engagement ring for you until the day we both put on a wedding band. We'll always wear them, just the way your grandmother's always worn hers."

"Hey, I thought there was no rush, that we were going to take our time and not leap into anything," Vivi protested, a teasing twinkle in her eyes, although the idea sounded wonderful to her. His willingness—eagerness!—to make a commitment was in such marvelous contrast to Barry.

He grinned a trifle ruefully. "I did say that, didn't I? We will. I meant it. But—in the meantime, you can wear a ring, can't you? You said once that you don't care for diamonds. It can be some other kind of stone, just as long as you wear it on the right hand."

"Somehow, a diamond doesn't seem nearly so hard and cold—not when it's given and worn with love," she said thoughtfully. "But, Marsh, rings are a big investment. Even simple ones don't come cheap. Shouldn't we wait—just a little bit?"

"Wait? I feel as if I've already waited a lifetime for you, and now I've got to wait till at least tomorrow, till this place opens, at the very soonest." He peered in, trying to see past the show window into the shop itself. "We would think of this on a Sunday! There aren't even any in the window."

He turned slightly to smile down at her. "I feel sure enough of our feelings to make the investment in our future—don't you?"

Vivi's fingers tightened in his and she leaned her face against his shoulder. "I don't really want to wait, either," she softly admitted. No matter what she'd suggested, his passionate answer was exactly what she wanted to hear.

"Then we will. You said you're staying on here to-night? We can come look at rings in the morning, in that case. Vivi, your job's done without you over a week already. Take a couple more days off. Come home with me to Paducah and see what you think of everything there."

"Tomorrow, yes—Paducah, no," Vivi sensibly compromised. "I don't need to see Paducah and your agency before deciding! If you're there, that's all that matters to me. I could enjoy living in the middle of the Sahara Desert, if you were there with me."

"Hold that thought," he quipped, grinning. "And when the time comes, do you suppose we could have the ceremony at your grandmother's house? It wouldn't be too much for her?"

"She'd love it. In fact, a few days ago she was telling me all about my parents' wedding there, and she was obviously itching for a repeat performance." Vivi laughed; everything seemed so marvelous this morning. "Oh, Marsh, for a minute, I thought you were going to suggest having the wedding on one of the bridges! And that reminds me, there's a painting of a certain bridge which I want to go buy after church."

"Our bridge?" He was quick to comprehend. "Your grandmother really should either give you away or be matron of honor. Bless her heart, she brought us together, didn't she?"

"She certainly did." Vivi's mind ranged ahead to thoughts of what a beautiful wedding that would be. "But I'm telling you right now, Marshall William Henderson, if we have the wedding at Gran's, *I'm* the one who's coming down those stairs. I don't trust you on them!"

"Just check them first for plastic spaceships," he

chuckled. With sudden apprehension, he glanced at the watch on his strong left wrist. "Hey, we'd better get to church. We don't want to be late!"

"No indeed," Vivi softly assented, and their eyes met in a long, loving gaze. "Not today of all days. We have so much to give thanks for!"

Promise Romances™ are available at your local bookstore or may be ordered directly from the publisher by sending $2.25 plus 75¢ (postage and handling) to the publisher for each book ordered.

If you are interested in joining Promise Romance™ Home Subscription Service, please check the appropriate box on the order form. We will be glad to send you more information and a copy of *The Love Letter,* the Promise Romance™ newsletter.

Send to: Etta Wilson
Thomas Nelson Publishers
P.O. Box 141000
Nashville, TN 37214-1000

☐ Yes! Please send me the Promise Romance titles I have checked on the back of this page.

I have enclosed _____ to cover the cost of the books ($2.25 each) ordered and 75¢ for postage and handling. Send check or money order. Allow four weeks for delivery.

☐ Yes! I am interested in learning more about the Promise Romance™ Home Subscription Service. Please send me more information and a *free* copy of *The Love Letter*.

Name _____

Address _____

City _____ State _____ Zip _____
Tennessee, California, and New York residents, please add applicable sales tax.

OTHER PROMISE ROMANCES ™
YOU WILL ENJOY

$2.25 each

Dear Reader:

I am committed to bringing you the kind of romantic novels you want to read. Please fill out the brief questionnaire below so we will know what you like most in Promise Romances™.

Mail to: Etta Wilson
Thomas Nelson Publishers
P.O. Box 141000
Nashville, Tenn. 37214-1000

1. Why did you buy this Promise Romance™?

   ☐ Author
   ☐ Back cover description
   ☐ Christian story
   ☐ Cover art
   ☐ Recommendation
      from others
   ☐ Title
   ☐ Other_____

2. What did you like best about this book?

   ☐ Heroine
   ☐ Hero
   ☐ Christian elements
   ☐ Setting
   ☐ Story line
   ☐ Secondary characters

3. Where did you buy this book?

   ☐ Christian bookstore
   ☐ Supermarket
   ☐ Drugstore
   ☐ General bookstore
   ☐ Home subscription
   ☐ Other (specify)_____

4. Are you interested in buying other Promise Romances_{TM}?

  ☐Very interested   ☐Somewhat interested
                ☐Not interested

5. Please indicate your age group.
    ☐Under 18   ☐25-34
    ☐18-24   ☐35-49   ☐Over 50

6. Comments or suggestions?

7. Would you like to receive a free copy of the Promise Romance_{TM} newsletter? If so, please fill in your name and address.

Name _____

Address _____

City _____ State _____ Zip _____

7371-4